BUNNY in a BASKET

Ben M. Baglio

Illustrations by Ann Baum

Cover illustration by
Mary Ann Lasher

AN
APPLE
PAPERBACK

SCHOLASTIC INC.

New York   Toronto   London   Auckland   Sydney
Mexico City   New Delhi   Hong Kong   Buenos Aires

Special thanks to Stephen Cole

ISBN 0-439-68761-6

12 11 10 9 8 7 6 5 4 3 2 1   5 6 7 8 9 10/0

Printed in the U.S.A.   40
First Scholastic printing, March 2005

One

"Look, there's another sign!" Mandy Hope exclaimed from the backseat of the Land Rover. "York — five miles."

"Move! Let me see," said her best friend, James Hunter, leaning over to peer through her window.

Mandy's dad, Dr. Adam Hope, slowed down as they neared their exit. "Anyone would think you two couldn't wait to get rid of me," he remarked.

"Anyone would think we were starting a week's vacation!" Mandy replied. She felt a tingle of excitement. "*That's* what we can't wait for! But I'll miss Animal Ark, too, of course." Right after breakfast that morning she had visited the residential unit at her parents' veterinary

1

practice to say good-bye to the animals — she knew they'd be well enough to go home before she got back next Saturday.

Mandy grinned at James as he polished his glasses on his T-shirt. They were going to stay with James's Aunt Mina and his cousin Nadia while his parents went on an Easter cruise around the Caribbean. Mandy thought James would have enjoyed a week in a place as beautiful as York, but to her surprise he'd practically begged her to come along with him for company.

"How about singing one more song before we get there?" Dr. Adam suggested as they passed a sign announcing that they had only four miles to go.

"Not another one!" Mandy gasped in mock dismay. Her ears were still ringing with her dad's rendition of "Ten Green Bottles" that seemed to have lasted most of the trip. "I hope you get the radio fixed before you come pick us up!"

"You should ask Nadia to fix it," grumbled James, pushing his glasses back onto his nose. "She'll probably just click her fingers and have it working in no time."

Dr. Adam frowned. "Is she good with electronic things?"

James sighed. "She's good at just about everything!"

Mandy gave him a sideways look. Nadia Hunter was twelve years old, the same age as Mandy, but she was a year ahead in school because she was considered advanced for her age. Mandy guessed that James got a little tired of his family always using Nadia as an example.

"Aha! So *that's* why you asked Mandy to come along, James," said Dr. Adam with a wink in the rearview mirror. "Safety in numbers, in case your perfect cousin tries to show you up!"

"It's not that," protested James. "It's just that Uncle Lionel's away working on the oil rig, and Nadia fills all her spare time with clubs and hobbies and extra lessons. Without Mandy there, I'd probably have nothing to do besides get under Aunt Mina's feet all week."

"Great!" said Mandy, nudging him in the ribs. "So I'm here just to keep you from getting bored?"

James looked defeated. "You *know* I didn't mean it like that!"

Mandy smiled again. You'd *better* not mean it like that! I'm missing some wonderful lambing time for this!"

"Yes, you are," said her dad, slowing down at a traffic light. "How will you cope without any animals for a week, Mandy?"

"She won't have to," said James. "In her last e-mail to me, Nadia said she'd gotten a rabbit."

"Awesome!" exclaimed Mandy. "What kind of rabbit? What's its name?"

"I can't remember," James admitted. "But knowing Nadia, it'll be the best-looked-after bunny in Yorkshire!"

Dr. Adam chuckled. "Well, I'm glad to hear it!"

"Me, too," said Mandy, her mood soaring. Even though it was only the first week in April, the sky was an unblemished blue, and the sunlight was so bright it dazzled her eyes. But James's face was still cloudy.

"Cheer up, James," said Mandy. "It's good of your aunt to take you in while your parents are away."

"Yes, it is," chimed in Dr. Adam, pulling away again into the lunchtime traffic. "If she'd said no, you'd be stuck in the Animal Ark residential unit for the week!"

Mandy laughed, and even James's face broke into a reluctant smile.

"I suppose I could have gone to stay with Blackie in the kennels," he joked. Blackie was his beloved black Labrador, and Mandy knew James was missing him already. "Actually, I still might end up there if Nadia or her mom try to make me do any folk dancing."

"Folk dancing?" Mandy echoed.

"Aunt Mina was a champ at it when she was growing up in Romania, before she came to England," James explained. "And of course, Nadia's been learning since she was old enough to walk." He looked anxiously at Mandy. "You won't let them make *me* learn any dances, will you?"

"Depends how busy I am playing with Nadia's rabbit," Mandy teased. "I bet you'd look great in one of those folk costumes."

"That's it!" wailed James. "Please, Dr. Adam, take me back to Welford — I'll bring my own water dish!"

Dr. Adam smiled. "Too late," he said, turning left. "This is your aunt's street. We made it!"

The Land Rover came to a stop outside an attractive townhouse on a quiet street. In spite of the threats about folk dancing, Mandy felt a twinge of anticipation.

"Come on, you two," said Dr. Adam. "Help me with the bags."

As Mandy and James clambered out and joined Dr. Adam at the back of the Land Rover, the front door opened to reveal a short, slim woman with tanned skin and friendly brown eyes.

"Hi, Aunt Mina!" called James, waving as he pulled out his backpack.

Mina Hunter smiled. "I thought I heard a car!" She spoke with only a faint trace of an Eastern European accent. "Welcome to you all!"

Mandy realized she'd been half expecting a woman in some kind of national dress, maybe with a headscarf or embroidered shawl. But Aunt Mina was well dressed in black trousers and a lilac long-sleeved top.

"Nadia!" she called back into the house. "Come on

down! James is here." She turned to Mandy and beamed. "And you must be Mandy."

"Nice to meet you," said Mandy. "This is my father."

"Adam Hope," added her dad, smiling and shaking hands. "I hope you won't have too much on your hands with these two."

"With my husband away, there's plenty of room for visitors," Aunt Mina replied. "Now, who would like some doughnuts and coffee?"

"Just the doughnuts for me, please!" said James, and Mandy nodded in agreement.

"I'd love to join in, but I'm afraid I have to get back," said Dr. Adam. "I'm meeting an old friend for lunch, and I think I'm a little late already."

"When you return for the children, then," Aunt Mina suggested. "Next week."

"That would be great." Dr. Adam grinned. "Bye, James. Bye, Mandy. Love you."

Mandy hugged him. "You, too, Dad. Give my love to Mom. See you next Saturday!"

Dr. Adam gave them a cheery wave and climbed back into the Land Rover. Mandy waved until he had vanished around the corner.

"Now," said Aunt Mina, "what about those doughnuts?"

"There's no time for that, Mom," came a girl's voice

from inside the house. "It's almost time to take Pixie to the show!"

Aunt Mina checked her watch. "Honestly, Nadia," she called back, "there is plenty of time. At least let James and Mandy unpack." She picked up Mandy's bag and James's backpack. "And come and say hello properly!"

Mandy followed James into the house. The hallway was as neat and good-looking as Aunt Mina, with warm biscuit-colored carpet and walls. In front of them and to the right, Mandy could see a sunny kitchen, while to their left a wooden door led to a spacious living room.

"I'll just get us something cold to drink," said Aunt Mina. "Then we'll show you to your rooms. James, you'll be staying in the spare room. Mandy, you'll be sharing with Nadia. Just a cot, I'm afraid, but it's really very comfy."

Mandy smiled. "I can sleep anywhere," she promised.

Aunt Mina looked pleased and went into the kitchen. Mandy then caught a glimpse of movement to her left. A dark-haired girl had appeared in the living room doorway. She was dressed in black jeans and a blue-and-white-striped top and had a pale, oval face with high cheekbones, framed by long curly hair. Her features were solemn and almost doll-like, with wide dark eyes and a snub nose.

"Hi, James," she said. "Long time, no see."

"Nadia!" James exclaimed. "I haven't seen you since Uncle Lionel's birthday last June. How are you?"

Nadia shrugged. "Busy. And you're Mandy, right? Hi. Good to meet you."

"Likewise," said Mandy. "Thanks for letting me share your room."

"That's OK." Nadia grinned unexpectedly. "But if you snore, I'll throw a pillow at your head!"

Mandy laughed. "Deal!"

"I'm sorry I can't hang around and chat," said Nadia, in the same way a busy teacher might politely dismiss some eager pupils, "but I really have to get Pixie ready. You'd better unpack quickly — we'll be going soon!" With that, she turned on her heel and disappeared back into the living room.

James rolled his eyes at Mandy. "See what I mean? She always acts like her life is busier and more important than anyone else's. But she's all right once you get to know her."

"She seems nice," said Mandy. "Just a bit distracted. Is Pixie her rabbit?"

James nodded. "Yes, I remember now."

Mandy followed Nadia into the living room. "I love rabbits. What's this about a show?"

Nadia was unlocking a set of patio doors at the far side of the room. "Can you bring Pixie's carrying case?" she asked, instead of answering Mandy's question. She pointed to a red-and-beige plastic case by the leather sofa and then flung open the door. "It's such a pretty day, I put Pixie out in his run!"

Mandy smiled and picked up the case, then followed James and Nadia out onto a small patio. Mandy's eyes opened wide as she looked out into the yard. "Look at that wall!" she cried. Made of old gray stone, it was easily as high as a two-story house.

"The yard backs onto the ancient city walls," James explained. "It's an amazing place to live, isn't it?"

"It is for Pixie, too," said Mandy, noticing a roomy wooden box nearby. The box was raised up on cinder blocks beneath a shady tree at the end of the garden. "That's not a hutch, it's a five-star rabbit hotel!" she declared. The living area was protected by wire mesh, while the nesting section was shielded by wood painted with colorful ivy and rambling roses. The roof was hinged to allow easy access. It had been covered with felt to keep the rain out, and lined with thin slate tiles so it wouldn't flap open in a strong wind.

"What did I tell you?" said James. "The best-looked-after rabbit in Yorkshire. In the world, probably."

Mandy smiled. "Let's take a look at him and see!"

Nadia was crouching over a large rabbit run in the middle of the lawn.

"Lucky old Pixie," Mandy remarked. "That run lets him nibble the lawn in this gorgeous yard, and he's got an amazing hutch to go back to when he's finished!"

Nadia nodded. "Dad built them both," she said. "I only decorated them. Could you open the carrying case for me, please?"

"Sure, I —" Mandy broke off in surprise. Up close, she could see that a line of brightly painted wooden flowers covered each side of the run, stretching up to the wire mesh roof. Even the wooden lid that offered Pixie shade was painted green with long orange flowers.

"Did you decorate this, too?" she asked.

Nadia gave her a brief, shy smile. "Mom said she didn't want an ugly old run cluttering up her garden. So I had to make it look pretty."

"It's terrific," said James, sounding genuinely impressed.

"Well, let's take a look at the lucky guy himself, shall we?" said Mandy, crouching down beside Nadia. She peered into the shady strip under the wooden lid. "Is he hiding in there?"

Nadia cleared her throat. "Uh, would you mind moving

back a bit? Pixie might feel crowded, and I don't want him to get nervous before the show."

Mandy looked at James and shrugged. "Sorry," she said as they both took a couple of steps back.

"Thanks." Nadia quietly opened up the painted lid. "Come on, Pixie," she cooed.

"You could offer him a treat to tempt him closer," Mandy suggested. "There's a plant he'd like over there. It's called groundsel."

"I think I can handle it, thanks," said Nadia.

"You should let Mandy pick him up," James suggested. "She knows lots about animals. Her parents are vets."

"Pixie doesn't really like strangers." She reached into the run again.

"Oh, come on, Nadia!" said James. "We're going to be here a whole week, so we won't be strangers for long, will we?"

Mandy nudged him and shook her head. Clearly, Nadia was very protective of her rabbit. Steaming in and trying to take over wasn't going to impress her one bit.

"Got you!" Nadia cried happily. "Mandy, James, this is Pixie." She pulled out a small rabbit, one hand cupped under his front legs and the other supporting his hindquarters. Pixie's black eyes blinked in the sudden sunlight. His coat was flecked with different shades of caramel and brown, and his incredibly long, floppy ears hung down on either side of his sweet little face. They almost came down to his tiny brown paws. His nose wrinkled as he sniffed the air and set his whiskers twitching.

"What a gorgeous agouti coat," Mandy said. "He's a Holland Lop, isn't he?"

Nadia blinked at her. "You really do know your animals, don't you?"

Mandy shrugged modestly. "Can I pet him?"

"I don't want to seem rude," said Nadia, "but Pixie really does get nervous with strangers. After the show, maybe?"

"Sure," said Mandy, turning red but trying to act undaunted. "Are you entering him in the class for lops?"

Nadia smiled knowingly. "It's not that sort of show. And if Pixie wins, the prize will be much better than just a ribbon!"

Mandy and James looked at each other.

"What kind of show is it?" James asked.

Just then, Aunt Mina poked her head out through the patio doors. "Doughnuts are in the kitchen," she called. "Ready when you are!"

"You go ahead," Nadia told them. "I'm going to give Pixie a last-minute grooming, and then we really have to leave for the chocolate factory."

James scratched his head. "The *chocolate* factory?"

"For a rabbit show?" Mandy exclaimed.

"It all makes perfect sense, really." Nadia grinned. "You'll see!"

"Come on, Mandy," said James, leading the way back to the house. "I'll bet Aunt Mina will tell us."

"I hope so," Mandy murmured. A rabbit show — in a chocolate factory? She had to admit, she was burning with curiosity!

Two

Half an hour later, Mandy and James were standing on the front steps watching Nadia settle Pixie's carrying case on the backseat of the car.

Mandy let out a contented sigh. "When your Aunt Mina talked about doughnuts, I thought she meant the sugary ones with a hole in the middle," she confessed. "I wasn't expecting a lunch of cottage cheese doughnuts with sour cream and jam!"

"I should have warned you," James smiled, licking his lips. "They're *papanazi*, a Romanian specialty. Aunt Mina's a fabulous cook."

"She sure is," Mandy agreed, frowning at a dark cloud edging into the sky. "You know, I think I might take my raincoat. Do you want yours? I can put it in my back-pack."

James smiled. "Thanks."

Once Mandy had stuffed the raincoats into her back-pack, she and James walked over to the car.

Nadia looked up as they approached. "How were the doughnuts?"

"Wonderful," said Mandy.

"I'm not so fond of them myself," said Nadia, a crafty smile spreading over her face. "I prefer *chocolate*."

"Here she goes again," groaned James.

Nadia acted innocent. "Oh, didn't Mom tell you about the show?"

"She couldn't," James said with a scowl. "She says you begged her to keep it a surprise!"

"Good old Mom." Nadia grinned. "It's a *great* surprise!"

Mandy found herself smiling. It was funny. Although Nadia acted bossy and reserved, there was something about her that Mandy warmed to. She obviously took her schoolwork and her hobbies very seriously, but there was a playful streak in her, too, that was hard not to like.

"OK," said Aunt Mina, coming out of the house. "I can't stand to keep quiet about this excursion any longer. Let's go!"

James got into the front seat while Mandy sat in the back with Nadia and Pixie. Nadia kept peeking at Pixie to check that he was OK in his basket, and Mandy couldn't resist a peek herself. The little rabbit, half hidden by hay, was keeping very still on a bed of newspaper. All Mandy could see of him was his caramel-and-chocolate hindquarters, gently quivering. She watched as Pixie raised a back leg to scratch himself behind his long floppy ears.

"Is he happy traveling in a car?" she asked.

"He normally doesn't mind," Nadia replied, "but he's been acting sort of funny lately."

"Oh?" said Mandy. "How?"

"Nothing really," said Nadia dismissively. "Hey, can you smell that? We're getting close!" She wound down the window and leaned out.

Mandy sniffed the air. Sure enough, a warm, rich scent was starting to fill the air. Chocolate!

"Merry's Chocolate Factory," Aunt Mina announced with a smile. "You can smell it a mile away!"

The smell grew stronger as they pulled up outside the factory. Signs advertising the show had been put up in the busy parking lot. Two teenage boys walked past, each carrying a cardboard box scored with airholes.

DOES YOUR RABBIT HAVE STAR QUALITY? asked one of

the signs. YOUR CHANCE TO OWN THE EASTER BUNNY! proclaimed another.

"All right, tell us, please," James begged. "What's this all about?"

Nadia leaned forward excitedly. "Every Easter, Merry's makes hollow chocolate rabbits and rabbit-shaped chocolate bars — their Easter bunny line."

Mandy nodded. "Mom always gets me one of the rabbits. They're delicious."

"Well, *this* year, Merry's wants to model their bunny after an actual local rabbit." Nadia explained. "And they'll put a picture of the winning rabbit on the chocolate wrapper and everything!"

"But Easter's next Sunday," James pointed out. "Won't it be over by the time the packaging is ready?"

"They have a new slogan," Nadia told him. "'Merry's Bunny brings you chocolate all year round!' So it's not just for Easter anymore."

"Wow," said Mandy. "Imagine Pixie staring out at you from all those chocolate bars!"

"There's more," Nadia went on. "Merry's will also make some life-size Easter bunnies out of chocolate. They're going to put them in special Easter baskets and give them to local charities as raffle prizes — and the owners of the winning bunny get to have one, too!"

"*That's* why my daughter is so distracted today." Aunt Mina smiled. "She's hoping for enough chocolate to last a whole year, all in the shape of one big bunny!"

"It would be amazing if Pixie won," said Mandy. "I can see why you're nervous."

"Imagine," said James dreamily. "A life-size Pixie made from solid chocolate."

"Well," said Mandy, "Pixie is just as sweet as chocolate already. I think he's got a really good chance of winning!"

"Thanks. I just hope the judges agree with you," said Nadia, biting her bottom lip and suddenly looking anxious.

From the parking lot, there were signs pointing the way to the hall where the judging would take place, though all they had to do was follow the trail of hopeful owners clutching cardboard boxes or carrying cases.

Finally, they came around a corner and saw a large single-story building decorated with Merry's flags and banners.

"That must be it," said James.

"Oh, dear," Nadia sighed. "This is even more nerve-racking than a dance competition!"

Once inside the hall, they joined the line of people waiting to be taken to their show tables.

"Look at all these rabbits!" Mandy gasped in delight.

It was a bit like a bunny-themed fair, she decided, except that instead of booths, there were tables covered with straw and shredded paper. And instead of things to sell, there were rabbits in all shapes and sizes! People were milling about everywhere, speaking in low voices, petting and grooming their rabbits. Ahead of them in the line, Mandy saw a girl holding a white French Lop, a young couple with a tortoiseshell Dutch, and a man with a Netherland Dwarf rabbit whose fur was, quite fittingly, chocolate colored.

"Pixie has some stiff competition," Aunt Mina observed, as if she could read Mandy's thoughts.

A curly-haired woman approached them with a clipboard. She was wearing a badge that said SUZIE, SHOW ASSISTANT. "Hello, there," she said with a warm smile. "Have you registered for the show?"

"Registered?" Nadia looked alarmed. "I sent in a form, if that's what you mean — *ages* ago."

"Our name is Hunter," said her mom more helpfully.

"Hunter, Hunter . . ." Suzie checked her clipboard and smiled down at the carrying case. "Then this must be Pixie!"

"Phew!" whistled Nadia. "Yes, it is!"

Suzie showed them to a table near the back of the hall. She gave Nadia a tag to write her name on and a piece of white paper so she could write down Pixie's name and breed.

"Good luck, dear," Suzie called as she bustled back across the busy hall to show the next group to their table.

Nadia opened the plastic door of the carrying case and gently scooped out Pixie. The small furry bundle looked around, his liquid black eyes shining.

"I hope he'll be OK when the judge holds him," said Nadia.

"Maybe you could let me hold him first," Mandy

suggested. "You know, to get him used to the idea of being with someone else."

Nadia looked deep in thought as she set down her rabbit and smoothed his ears. "All right," she decided.

Carefully, Mandy lifted the little ball of warm fur and cradled him against her chest. Pixie peeped over her fingers to cast shy glances around the room, his nose twitching. Mandy stroked his velvety ears, and her fingers brushed against his quivering whiskers. He looked up at her, then stretched out his neck and bobbed his head as if nodding good afternoon.

"You're gorgeous, aren't you, little one?" Mandy cooed. "You're going to wow the judges!"

Nadia was looking a little uncomfortable. "Can I have him back now, please? I want to settle him down before the judging starts."

"Thanks for letting me hold him," Mandy said, handing Pixie back to her.

"Come on," said James. "Let's look around the hall."

"Leave your bag here, Mandy," suggested Aunt Mina. "We'll watch it."

"Thanks," said Mandy.

As they made their way through the rows of tables, an electronic squeal buzzed out over speakers that were placed around a makeshift stage. Suzie was standing on the stage. She cautiously tapped the microphone and cleared her throat.

"The first round of judging will begin shortly," she announced. An excited murmur ran through the crowd. "The judges will visit each table before drawing up a short list for the final judging."

"It'll take ages to get through this bunch of bunnies," James remarked.

"They have quite a few judges by the look of it," said Mandy. Several men and women with blue badges on their chests were moving purposefully to different parts of the hall. "And look, James. That must be one of the special baskets for the winning chocolate bunny!"

A man in brown overalls was carrying a large wicker basket onto the stage. It was decorated with bright yellow-and-orange ribbons and lined with straw.

"I bet that's the throne for whichever rabbit wins!" James guessed.

"Probably. It's a very grand basket," Mandy agreed.

But James was no longer looking at the stage. "Hey, Mandy," he said. "Look at that incredible ball of fluff!"

Mandy grinned as she followed James over to a pure white angora who was seated on a black velvet cushion. Pink eyes and an even pinker nose stood out from its fluffy face. A girl about Mandy's age stood next to the table. She was very pretty, and from the way she was posing with her rabbit, she clearly knew it. She seemed as perfectly groomed as her pet, with blond hair so long that it almost reached to her waist.

Mandy smiled at the girl. "He's adorable!"

"He is a *she*," the girl corrected her. "This is Princess Powderpuff. She's bound to win, don't you think?"

"I'm sure she's got a good chance," Mandy said politely. "I guess it depends on what the judges are looking for."

"Oh, they'll be looking for my precious puff ball, just you wait," the girl replied, patting the velvet cushion. "Black shows her off best, don't you think? We Angells really know how to coordinate."

James frowned. "Did you just call yourself an *angel*?"

"It's my name, silly. Angelica Angell," she explained. "I can't imagine why no one else brought along a special cushion for their rabbit. No sense of style, I suppose."

Mandy and James swapped a glance and quickly moved on.

"I think Princess Powderpuff would make a terrible Easter bunny," James muttered once they were out of earshot. "If she's anything like her owner, she'd be too busy admiring herself to hand out eggs."

Mandy swallowed a burst of laughter in case Angelica was watching them.

"Come on, Alf," someone said behind them. "If you want to win, they've got to be able to see you."

Mandy turned at the sound of the plaintive voice and saw a slender young woman with frizzy red curls kneeling in front of a carrying case. A dark-haired man hovered nearby, looking very worried.

"She just hates her case." He sighed. "I knew this would happen."

"Do you have that alfalfa, Barry?" asked the woman. She noticed Mandy and James watching and gave them a grin. "It's Alf's favorite, so I named her after it."

Barry handed the woman a few sprigs of a cloverlike plant. "Here, Rachel. Let's hope it works."

Mandy crouched beside Rachel and saw an adorable dark blue dwarf rabbit huddled inside a tangle of straw. Alf's large brown eyes were wide open, and unlike Pixie's, her short velvety ears stood straight up from her head. Her pink nose twitched as she slowly crept forward, enticed by the smell of her favorite food.

"It's working," whispered Mandy. "Good for you!"

"Barry Greenhalgh, I've caught you!" said a deep-voiced, jolly-looking man. Mandy saw from his badge that he was one of the judges. "You know Merry's workers aren't allowed to enter the show!"

"True, Mr. Northington." Barry smiled. "But there's nothing that says my next-door neighbor can't enter, is there? Even if she *is* my girlfriend."

"Good luck, Alf," Mandy murmured as Rachel scooped up the little rabbit in both hands.

"I'm not sure Alf's really Easter bunny material," Rachel admitted. "She's not the liveliest of rabbits, by any means. But it would be a real thrill if she *did* win!"

With a wink at Mandy, she stood up and put Alf on the table. Barry Greenhalgh stepped aside to let Mr. Northington through for his inspection.

"Do you know the rabbit judge?" James asked him.

"He's not a rabbit judge," said Barry, chuckling. "He's my supervisor at the factory!"

"So how come he's here?" Mandy wondered. "I mean, he's judging, right?"

"Yes, but it's not like a real show," Barry explained. "All the judges are senior staff here at Merry's. They're looking for three things in these Easter bunny wannabes — looks, fun, and tons of character."

Mandy looked around. "But these rabbits are *all* so pretty. How can they decide?"

"The judges give each rabbit up to ten points for different categories," said Barry, "and the scores are added up. If there's a tie, the final choice is made by Jenny Maynard, the boss's wife. This competition was her idea."

"Well, I hope Alf does well," said Mandy.

"Thanks, kid!" Barry grinned. "And good luck yourself. May the best bunny win!"

Just then Mandy noticed a small commotion two tables away from Alfalfa. A lively gray rabbit was not enjoying the judge's attention. He was trying to wriggle free, thumping his back legs on the table and sending scraps of torn paper and wood shavings flying over his startled owner.

Acting on instinct, Mandy went over to the table and placed one palm firmly on the rabbit's hindquarters. The surprised judge stood back to let her take over. Mandy stroked the rabbit's head and ears with her free hand, murmuring soothing noises, and soon the rabbit was sitting quietly.

"You've got a real knack for bunnies!" The judge smiled. "Care to help me with some more contestants?"

"I'd love to!" Mandy exclaimed.

James had already reached the next table, where two black rabbits sat crunching on opposite ends of the same carrot. "They're Roly and Poly," James reported, reading their name cards.

Mandy held Roly first, then held Poly steady while the judge made notes on her clipboard. Mandy was dying to know what she was writing. Had a winner already been decided?

"Let's check on Pixie," James suggested when the judge moved on to the next rabbit, a very sleepy-looking black-and-white doe. Together they made their way back over to Pixie's table.

"Well, the judge has made a decision," Aunt Mina told them. "There's nothing more we can do except hope!"

"He was good as gold," Nadia said proudly. "Weren't you, Pixie?" She smiled at Mandy. "Would you like another turn petting him?"

"I'd love one!" Mandy smiled at the sweet little lop and gently ran her hand over his amazing ears. The rabbit nuzzled the top of his head into her palm, half closing his eyes in contentment.

"I'll bet Angelica Angell didn't like the judge cuddling her 'precious puff ball,'" James remarked, making a face.

"Oh, no!" Nadia rolled her eyes. "*She's* not here, is she?"

Mandy frowned. "You know her?"

"I wish I didn't!" Nadia said with feeling. "She's in the class ahead of me at school, and she's *so* full of herself." She stuck her nose in the air and delivered a good impression of Angelica's snooty voice. "'My daddy drives *such* a fast car, and Mommy runs an exclusive little boutique in the center of York, you know!'"

"Now, now, Nadia," her mother chided her, trying to hide a smile.

Just then, there were some taps on the microphone, and the hall became quiet. Mandy saw that a smiling woman in a white blouse and checked skirt had climbed onto the stage.

"A big hello to you all, and thank you for taking part in our competition today," she began. "I'm Jenny Maynard, and my husband, Sam, is the head chocolate maker here at Merry's. He'll soon be making a chocolate replica of one lucky rabbit — a rabbit who is in this room even as we speak!"

A few excited "oohs" rose up from the audience, along with a small round of applause. But suddenly, the clapping stopped, and people by the door started pointing and yelling.

"What's happening?" cried Nadia.

"Look!" shouted James. "There's a dog in here! Oh, no, the rabbits!"

Mandy saw what was going on at that same moment. A large, glossy-coated Irish setter had found its way into the hall full of helpless bunnies!

Three

Mandy watched in dismay as the Irish setter darted around the hall. At first it raced in a wide circle, barking excitedly. Then it skidded to a halt, wagging its tail, and jumped up at one of the show tables with such force the table almost toppled over. The man beside it yelled and grabbed his rabbit, and the setter jumped back in surprise.

"Herring!" Jenny Maynard shouted into the microphone. "Herring, stop that at once!"

If anything, her booming voice caused even more panic. All around the hall, frightened rabbits were scrabbling across the tables or leaping out of their

owners' arms. Trying to move out of the dog's way, people knocked into one another or bumped against the tables. Mr. Northington lunged for Herring, but the setter was too fast and dodged out of the way.

Meanwhile, Angelica Angell had climbed up onto a table. She was clutching Princess Powderpuff to her chest and screaming at the top of her lungs. Herring's ears flattened as if to try and shut out the terrible din, and Mandy saw that his eyes were stretched wide with fear.

"She's making things worse," Nadia wailed, holding Pixie tightly.

"*Really*, Herring!" shouted Jenny Maynard. She got down from the stage and launched herself into the confused crowd.

James gasped and grabbed Mandy's arm. "Roly and Poly!" he shouted. "Look, they're on the ground! They might get squashed!"

Mandy saw the little black bundles cowering under a table while their distraught owners searched frantically in the wrong direction. "Pick them up, James!" she cried. "I'll get Herring!"

The dog was already bounding toward her. By now he looked as frightened as the rabbits by all the shouting and crashing around. While other people scrambled out of the setter's way and Angelica shrieked even louder, Mandy stepped forward to block his path.

"Herring," she said in a commanding voice. "Stay!"

The crowd around her fell quiet. Herring skittered to a halt in the middle of the hall, holding his head on one side. His ears twitched, and he looked ready to dart off again when Barry Greenhalgh crept up behind him and grabbed his collar. Herring strained to get away, his claws scrabbling on the wooden floor, but Barry had a good hold.

"It's OK, Herring," Mandy said, looking into the dog's worried black eyes. She placed a hand firmly on his back, encouraging him to sit while she looked around for James.

"It's all right!" James called. He was on his knees beside an overturned table and raised his hands to reveal a small black rabbit in each.

The hall was still noisy, and it seemed like many rabbits were still on the loose. But now that Herring had stopped tearing around, everyone calmed down and concentrated on retrieving their pets. Mandy crouched in front of the dog, murmuring calming words. She stroked his smooth head, running her fingers through the rich rust-red of his glossy coat. After a few moments, Herring flopped down on the polished hall floor, panting with his mouth open in a broad doggy grin.

"That was good work," said Barry, beaming.

"Oh, Herring," Jenny Maynard said breathlessly. "Thanks for getting hold of him, Barry. And a special thank you to *you*, Miss . . . ?"

"Mandy Hope," said Mandy. "Pleased to meet you."

"Well, I'm sorry you had to meet my disobedient dog!" Jenny Maynard sighed and wiped her forehead with a handkerchief. "He must have escaped from my husband's office and followed my trail here. If only he could follow *commands* so well!"

Herring looked up at her quizzically. His ears were still flat against his head, and his russet tail thumped against the floor.

"Yes, you know I'm upset with you, don't you?" she

said. "But I'm really angry with myself. Look at this chaos. It's all my fault!"

"Ow!" cried a small boy close by, quickly putting his rabbit down on the table. "Bingo bit me! Look!" The boy started to cry and was comforted by his mother while his father looked angrily in Herring's direction.

Jenny looked at Mandy. "Herring seems happy to stay with you for the moment. Could you watch him while I try to calm things down?"

"Of course," Mandy answered, tousling Herring behind the ear. "Good luck!"

James came back over and let out a low whistle of relief. "Wow, Mandy, you did a great job there."

"You did well yourself, finding those lost rabbits," said Barry, and James blushed. "Come on, let's help round up a few more."

"OK." James nodded and set off after him. As he passed Angelica, who was still standing on the table with Princess Powderpuff, she tapped him on the shoulder with her foot.

"Will you please help us down?" In her shrill voice, it sounded more like a command than a request.

"Oh, er, yes," said James, shooting a frustrated glance at Mandy.

He reached up and took hold of the white rabbit while Barry helped Angelica down to the floor. Herring was watching, too, and let out a loud bark. With a startled shriek, Angelica pulled away from Barry and toppled over, landing in an undignified heap under the table. Mandy heard Nadia snort with laughter and tried to hide her own smile.

"That dog should be put to sleep!" Angelica snarled. "It's completely wild!"

Mandy gave her a cold look but was alarmed to see a few people nodding in agreement.

"May I have your attention, please, ladies and gentlemen, boys, girls, and bunnies," said Jenny Maynard as she climbed back onstage. "I cannot apologize enough for that, uh, unexpected appearance by my dog, Herring. I want to make it quite clear that he is *not* one of the official judges!"

There was a ripple of weak laughter at her joke, but a lot of people were still muttering angrily.

"I understand that your rabbits have been upset by the disturbance and will not be at their best," she went on. "So I'd like to postpone the next round of judging until everyone's had a chance to calm down and tidy up."

There was a groan from the crowd. Herring began to whine, as if he could sense the unhappy atmosphere. Mandy shushed him by stroking his flank, and he licked her hand.

"I know you're disappointed, and believe me, so are

all of us at Merry's," said Jenny Maynard. "If we're going
to have our new bunny chocolate mold ready in time
for Easter, we need to move fast. So, now I would like
to read out the names of the twenty lucky rabbits who
have made it through the first round and into the finals
on" — she turned to Suzie the show assistant for confir-
mation — "Wednesday evening at six o'clock."

A tide of chatter and whispers swept around the hall
as people excitedly checked their schedules to make
sure they could come if their pet was one of the chosen
few. Looking around, she saw James and Barry at the
back of the hall. They were still on their hands and
knees, clearly in pursuit of another bunny.

"And one more thing," said Jenny Maynard. "To show
you how much we appreciate your bringing your rabbits down to the factory today, and how sorry I am for
our unexpected interruption, I'd like to offer each of
you a small thank-you present." There was a twinkle in
her blue eyes. "Each rabbit's owners should see Suzie
on the way out so that she can present you with a special selection of Merry's chocolates!"

Mandy wasn't surprised that this announcement was
greeted with a much warmer round of applause. Only
Angelica kept a scowl on her face, as if she thought that
Princess Powderpuff should be awarded first prize then
and there.

Just then, Mandy noticed Barry's girlfriend, Rachel, looking upset. She was bending down and peering around on the floor. Mandy had a sudden dreadful feeling. She hoped nothing had happened to poor, timid little Alf.

"Now, I am happy to announce the twenty finalists for the Merry's Easter Bunny," Jenny Maynard announced as Suzie handed her a clipboard. "Beautiful bunnies with lively, sparkling personalities that bring a smile to everyone's face, just like Merry's chocolate!" She paused for some polite laughter from the crowd, then began to read the list aloud. "On Wednesday evening, the rabbits we'd *love* to see again are . . . Scruff," a small chorus of cheers went up, "Twitcher," another cheer, and a ripple of applause, "Nelson . . ."

But Mandy was barely listening now. She could see Rachel peering inside an overturned cardboard box, then, more desperately, under a baseball cap. Was Alf missing? Mandy wished she could help, but she didn't dare leave Herring. With her fingers curled securely around the setter's collar, she waved frantically with her free hand toward James. He finally looked up, and she pointed over to Rachel, indicating they should go and see her. James nodded and held up a finger to suggest he'd be there in a minute.

"Britney, Maisie . . ." Jenny Maynard paused for the

applause and looked up with a frown. "Jellyfish?" An excited boy near the front started jumping up and down, and she grinned. "Jellyfish the rabbit — fair enough! Now, who else do we have? Douglas, Murgatroyd, Princess Powderpuff . . ."

"Yes!" screeched Angelica. "I knew it! I knew it!"

"Fluffnose," Jenny Maynard continued, "Coppertail, Pixie . . ."

"Go, Pixie!" whooped Nadia. She and her mother high-fived, and Mandy flashed them an excited smile. But she was feeling more and more anxious about Alf, which spoiled her happiness for Pixie making it to the final round. She saw Barry crossing over to Rachel. He looked crestfallen as he gathered her up in a warm hug.

"And a short name to finish on," proclaimed Jenny Maynard, "Alf!" Barry and Rachel looked up, their faces very pale. Mandy's stomach did a somersault. The little rabbit had done so well — but where was she?

"That's it, ladies and gentlemen," said Jenny Maynard. "Thank you all so much. I hope to see the top twenty rabbits back here on Wednesday."

As people started to file out from the hall, Nadia rushed over to Mandy. "Isn't it great?" she said. "Pixie's made it into the top twenty!"

"It's fantastic," Mandy agreed.

But then James came over, looking serious. "Barry

and I helped locate three more rabbits," he said, "but Alf's nowhere to be found!"

Mandy bit her lip. "As soon as Mrs. Maynard's back, I'll help you search," she promised.

Jenny Maynard was already making her way over to the middle of the hall. "Phew!" she said. "Well, I think we managed to rescue the situation, eh, Herring?" She clipped a leash to his collar. "Thank you again for calming him down."

"No problem," said Mandy.

As soon as Herring's leash was on, he jumped up, wagging his plumy red tail. "Oh, dear," said Jenny Maynard, sighing. "Now he thinks it's time for a walk. Trouble is, he also thinks that *he* is walking *me*! Bye!"

Mandy waved good-bye to them as Herring tugged his owner toward the hall door. Then she and James followed Nadia back to Pixie's show table.

Aunt Mina was bending down to get Mandy's backpack from under a nearby chair. "There you are, Mandy the dog tamer!" She smiled, passing her the backpack. "I think someone kicked it over in all the excitement. Well, we'd better get going."

"Hang on," said James, frowning. "Alf is still missing, and we were going to help look for her."

Aunt Mina shook her head. "I'm really sorry, but Nadia has a folk-dancing lesson in an hour."

Nadia looked at her mom. "Can't we stay just five more minutes? I'd love to help, and it won't matter if I'm a tiny bit late."

Aunt Mina checked her watch, then sighed and nodded. "All right. Hand me Pixie." Nadia carefully passed the agouti rabbit over to her mother. He snuggled down with his beady black eyes half closed, like he was sleepy. "I'll put him back in his carrying case," she said. "Good luck!"

Mandy and James described Alf to Nadia, and she joined in the search, which grew easier as families filed out of the hall to collect their free chocolate. Mandy and James paused briefly to say good-bye to Roly and Poly and their owners. But when the five minutes were up, neither they nor Barry and Rachel had had any luck. There was no sign of a tiny dark blue rabbit anywhere.

Nadia sighed. "I'm really sorry we have to go," she said.

James turned to Barry and Rachel. "I hope you find Alf soon."

Rachel nodded and wiped her eyes. "She has to be here somewhere. She may be small, but she can't just vanish!"

"Thanks for helping, anyway," said Barry. "If she doesn't show up soon, I'll get some of my friends to help us. We'll find her, don't worry."

Mandy's heart went out to them both. "I'm sure we'll see you all on Wednesday for the last round," she said, swinging her backpack onto her shoulder. "Bye!"

She followed James and Nadia back to where Aunt Mina stood waiting.

"I just don't get it," James said. "Remember when vandals messed up Woodbridge Park Farm and the rabbits and guinea pigs got out? We found them all, even though some had gotten miles away. And now we can't find one rabbit in a little hall like this."

"Maybe when the hall is completely empty, Alf will think it's safe to come out," said Mandy, adjusting the strap on her backpack. "We'll just have to hope that Barry's friends have better luck than we did."

They didn't have time to line up for their free chocolate samples, but no one felt very hungry, anyway. On the way home, Aunt Mina tried to raise their spirits by reminding them of how well Pixie did.

"In a funny way, I almost wish Pixie hadn't made the top twenty," sighed Nadia. "The next round is going to be even *more* nerve-racking."

"Pixie's a star," Mandy told her, stroking the little rabbit's silky-soft fur through the cage. "I'm sure he'll do well."

Once they were back at the house, Nadia placed Pixie in his hutch, then raced upstairs to change for her dance class. Mandy and James lingered in the hall.

"So," Aunt Mina said, and smiled at them. "What about you two?"

"Er . . ." James looked pale. "I — I don't have the right shoes to go dancing."

"I don't expect you to join in the lesson." His aunt laughed. "But you can come along and wait, or you can stay here — we'll only be gone about an hour."

"I haven't unpacked yet," Mandy said. "I can do that."

"Good idea," Aunt Mina agreed.

Mandy crouched down beside her backpack and pulled out her raincoat. "We didn't need our rain gear after all, did we?" she remarked.

"It was good to be prepared, though," said James. "You never know what to expect in April."

Suddenly, Mandy gasped, staring down at her bag. "You can say that again! Look!"

There, curled up in James's jacket, was a tiny blue-black dwarf rabbit. It was Alf!

Four

"No wonder we couldn't find Alf," Mandy cried. "She'd already found us!"

"Goodness!" exclaimed Aunt Mina. "You brought home a stowaway."

"She must have hopped off the table and into my bag in all the confusion," Mandy realized. Carefully, she reached in and retrieved the little rabbit. Alf's lustrous fur felt warm and soft as she sat quietly in Mandy's palm. "I bet it was nice and cozy in my bag — just the place to escape to."

James's grin stretched from ear to ear. "Wait till we

tell Barry and Rachel!" Then his face fell. "Wait — how *can* we tell them? We don't know how to contact them."

"Barry works at the factory," Mandy remembered. "We can contact him there."

"But it's Saturday, and he won't be there till Monday," said James. "He and Rachel will be really upset, wondering what's happened to Alf all that time."

"Wait a minute," said Aunt Mina. "Jenny Maynard organized the competition. I'm sure we sent the registration forms to her address. Perhaps we can get her number out of the phone book. If Barry works for her, she must know how to reach him."

"Great idea," said Mandy. She turned to call upstairs. "Hey, Nadia! Look who's come to visit Pixie!"

"What are you talking about?" said Nadia. When she appeared at the top of the stairs, both Mandy and James were slightly taken aback. She had changed into a white blouse decorated with colorful embroidered flowers, and in place of her jeans she wore a long, black wool skirt. Her hair was hidden by a black headscarf threaded with silver braid, and on her feet she wore a pair of plain leather sandals.

"You look amazing!" said Mandy.

"Never mind me," said Nadia, rushing downstairs. "Is that *Alf* you're holding?"

James nodded. "Mandy kidnapped her!"

"I did not," Mandy protested. She let Nadia take Alf.

"She's so sweet," cooed Nadia. "Almost as pretty as Pixie!"

"Come on, Nadia, we're late enough as it is," said Aunt Mina. "Mandy, I promise I'll find Mrs. Maynard's address when we get back. Then we can see about getting Alf back home."

"What are we going to do with her until then?" asked Nadia, passing Alf back to Mandy. "If we put her in with Pixie they might fight or something."

"A doe and a buck usually get along fine," said Mandy. "But if Pixie's in his hutch, maybe Alf could borrow his run for now?"

"Good idea," said Aunt Mina.

"We can play with the rabbits until you get back," said James, looking pleased.

"I'd rather you didn't play with Pixie," Nadia said bossily as she handed Alf back to Mandy. "He's had a very busy day."

"Oh, OK," said Mandy, raising her eyebrows at James. She'd forgotten how possessive Nadia could be about her rabbit.

"Help yourself to juice in the fridge, and there are plenty of videos you can watch," called Aunt Mina as she and Nadia vanished through the door. "Bye for now!"

The door slammed shut, and Mandy held Alf closer. "Don't worry," she murmured. "It'll be a lot quieter around here for a while."

"Nadia's so sensitive about Pixie," said James, sighing.

"She just loves him to pieces, that's all," said Mandy. "Come on, Alf. Let's make your stay here as comfortable as we can."

When they went out through the patio doors, the sun was still shining despite the few dark clouds spotting the sky. Pixie was sitting in his living area with his nose against the wire mesh as if he was curious about the visitor, but Mandy was true to her word and didn't disturb him.

James lifted up one side of the run, and Mandy put Alf inside. The rabbit stayed very still for a few moments, then scampered with funny little hops over to the shady strip under the lid.

"She probably feels more secure there," said Mandy.

"It's a shame Pixie doesn't have a spare water bottle," said James. "Can we give her a saucer of water or something?"

"Well, a water dish wouldn't be a good idea if she was in a hutch," said Mandy. "It could overturn and leave her floor damp. But out here it should be fine."

James nodded. "I'll figure something out."

"I'll see if I can find her some alfalfa," said Mandy,

looking around the garden. "It might make her a bit happier if we can give her some of her favorite food."

She couldn't find alfalfa anywhere, but she pulled some weeds from a corner of the garden and poked them through the wire to see if Alf would be interested.

"One saucer of water," James announced behind her.

Mandy was about to lift up the run so he could place it inside when she froze. "Don't move," she whispered to James. "Look!"

Slowly, her pink nose sniffing the air, Alf emerged from the shade and hopped toward the plants. She paused uncertainly, her short, perky ears pointing skyward. After a few more moments she scampered over to the weeds and started to nibble, timidly at first, then with growing interest.

"That's it, Alf," Mandy whispered.

The little rabbit soon moved to another pile, nibbling with the same enthusiasm.

"Hey, it's not fair that Alf gets all those tasty treats," said James. "I know we can't play with Pixie, but at least we could give him some food."

"Good idea," said Mandy. "I'm sure Nadia wouldn't mind us treating her bunny just this once."

Once she'd lifted up the run to allow James to slide the saucer of water inside, they walked over to Pixie's hutch and poked some leafy stems through the wire of his living area. Mandy noticed some carrot slices and cabbage lying untouched by his dry-food bowl. "Perhaps he'll like these as a change," she murmured. "Rabbits are like humans. They need variety in their diets so they don't get bored."

"If those Romanian doughnuts were anything to go by, we'll be getting plenty of variety ourselves this week," said James, patting his stomach. "I wonder what we're having for supper."

The time passed quickly for Mandy and James as they watched the two rabbits. Pixie kept coming up to the front of his cage to sniff Mandy's finger, moving his head this way and that.

"He's almost more interested in your finger than in the plants," James joked.

Soon, Nadia and her mother were calling "hello" through the front door, and Nadia came right out to see them in the backyard.

"Good class?" Mandy asked.

"It went much slower than usual," said Nadia, her cheeks still a little red with effort. "We did the *Paparuda*, but I kept thinking about Alf and Pixie and my feet got all messed up!" She marched over to the run. "How is Alf doing?"

"She's eating her way through a stack of weeds,"

Mandy announced cheerily as she and James followed behind.

"We gave some to Pixie, too, so he wouldn't feel left out," James added. "We poked them through his cage. We didn't lift up the roof or disturb him."

Nadia nodded and seemed pleased. "Thanks."

The three of them watched Alf finish off the last of the weeds.

"She won't stay dwarf-sized for long if she eats like that," grinned Nadia. "She'll be a giant!"

Just then, Aunt Mina appeared at the patio doors. "I have Jenny Maynard's address," she called. "She lives on the Yarrow estate, but unfortunately her phone number isn't listed. We'll have to drive over there." She gave a theatrical sigh. "All this to and fro . . . I'll be glad to have a rest!"

"It will be worth it when we take Alf back to Barry and Rachel," Mandy promised, glancing down at the sweet little dark blue shape in Pixie's run. They must be going out of their mind with worry, but it wouldn't be too long before they were reunited with their pet.

As soon as Nadia had changed out of her dance clothes, they all piled back into the car.

"I wonder if Jenny Maynard will let us play with Herring while we're there," said James.

Mandy looked at him sympathetically. "You miss Blackie, don't you?"

James sighed and nodded. "I know I just saw him this morning, but it feels like ages ago!"

"Well, a lot's happened since this morning," Mandy reminded him.

"That's the road, Mom," said Nadia, pointing. "Greenway. Mrs. Maynard lives at number fifty-six."

Aunt Mina turned left onto a pleasant, shady avenue lined with silver birches. Number 56 was set back from the road. A long driveway snaked behind some glossy dark green bushes that had been trimmed into leafy pyramids and obelisks.

"We'll go and ask her for Barry's address," announced Nadia. "Wait here, Mom."

"I'll turn the car around," Aunt Mina told them.

Mandy and James followed Nadia along the driveway. The house was large and covered with ivy. Nadia knocked loudly on the green front door. A minute or so later, she tried again. But there was no reply.

"Uh-oh," said Mandy. "They must be out."

"We can come back tomorrow by ourselves, first thing," said Nadia. "It's only a mile or so from my house. Not such a long walk, and nice and quiet, too."

"Good idea," said Mandy.

"Well, there's nothing more we can do now," Nadia

said briskly. "Let's go home for some supper. Alf can sleep in Pixie's carrying case tonight."

"Oh — she might not like that," Mandy said worriedly. "Barry said she hated carrying cases. She only feels happy in her hutch."

"It's only for one night," said Nadia.

But back home, when they tried to put Alf inside the carrying case, she scampered right back out again and sat on the grass, shivering. Mandy saw that the rabbit's big chocolate-brown eyes were wide with fright. She picked up Alf and cradled her, and the bunny snuggled in the crook of her arm.

"Can't Alf just share Pixie's hutch for the night?" suggested James.

"Pixie has never shared before," said Nadia. "He might not like a strange rabbit invading his space."

"We could make a divider," said James. "A wide strip of cardboard, dividing the hutch in two. Pixie can have one half and Alf the other."

"That should work." Mandy turned to Nadia. "After all, it's only for a night, isn't it?"

"All right," said Nadia. "I'll clear out half of Pixie's hutch and put down some fresh bedding. I'm sure Mom has an old cardboard box we can cut up."

"Thanks, Nadia," Mandy said, and beamed.

"We'll get up early tomorrow and see Mrs. Maynard,"

said James. "If she can put us in touch with Barry right away, Alf could be home by lunchtime."

Mandy was woken the next morning by Nadia bumping against the cot as she got dressed. The sun was streaming in through the yellow curtains, casting bright patches of light on the bare orange walls. All Nadia's pictures were stuck onto two large bulletin boards, practically invisible behind an assortment of posters and pictures of everything from horses and rabbits to ballet dancers.

"Did you sleep OK?" Nadia asked, pulling on a black sweater.

"Yes, the bed's really comfortable." Mandy yawned, stretching her arms. "I didn't snore, did I?"

"Luckily for you, no," answered Nadia. "Otherwise I might have built a divider like the one in Pixie's hutch!"

Mandy laughed. "What time is it?"

"It's seven-thirty," said Nadia. "Time to go. I've already woken James."

"Bet that wasn't easy," said Mandy.

Nadia giggled. "Like trying to raise the *Titanic*!"

"Let's see if waking the rabbits is any easier," Mandy said.

But when they went into the garden, Nadia made a discovery that seemed to spoil her good mood.

"Look!" she complained. "Alf might be small, but she's stronger than we thought."

The divider in Pixie's hutch had been pushed down during the night. Alf had clambered across from her own side and was in Pixie's living space, nibbling on a sunflower seed while Pixie watched from the doorway to his sleeping area.

Anxiously, Nadia picked up her rabbit, checking him for scratches or signs of a fight, while Mandy studied Alf.

"This little one seems fine," she reported. "How's Pixie?"

"I can't *see* any problems," Nadia admitted. But when she stroked the side of Pixie's face, the rabbit pulled sharply away. "He's upset," she said, and sighed. "Alf crashing through must have really frightened him."

"He's eaten his food," Mandy noticed. "So he can't be too upset."

"Alf probably ate it for him," Nadia said huffily.

"Oh, dear, Alf," said Mandy. "Looks like you've gone from being in a rabbit hutch to being in the doghouse."

She carried Alf back to the run, and Nadia put Pixie in his carrying case while she cleaned out his hutch. James came downstairs just as she was finishing up. She and Mandy explained to him what had happened.

"They probably had a really nice time together," James ventured.

"I think I know my rabbit best," snapped Nadia.

Mandy shrugged. "Alf didn't know she was doing anything wrong," she pointed out. "Do you still want to come to Mrs. Maynard's with us?"

Nadia nodded. "Of course, I do. I'm sorry I got upset. It's just that I love Pixie so much. I get very protective of him." She looked at Pixie, huddled up in a quiet little ball in his case. "Oh, well, I'm sure he'll cheer up soon. I'll just pop Pixie back. We'll have some breakfast, and then get going, OK?"

"Sounds good," said Mandy.

"Should we take Alf with us?" asked James.

Mandy considered. "It's a long way to carry him," she said. "We'd better leave him in the run."

After they'd devoured some hot buttered toast, Nadia led them out into the quiet sunlit street. In spite of the mix-up with the rabbits' sleeping arrangements, Mandy felt a real spring in her step. The dark clouds that had threatened rain the day before had boiled away; today the blue sky boasted nothing but a few fluffy wisps of brilliant white. And best of all, soon, if all went well, Alf would be reunited with his owners.

Five

They reached the Maynards' house a little after nine o'clock. This time, when Nadia knocked, a frantic barking started up.

"Fingers crossed they're home," said James.

After a few moments the door half opened and Jenny Maynard peered out, dressed in a white terry cloth robe. Mandy glimpsed Herring bouncing up and down behind her, trying to see who had come to call.

"May I help you?" Jenny Maynard said politely. "Wait a moment — it's Mandy, isn't it? You were at the hall yesterday, helping with Herring."

Mandy grinned at her. "That's right. He looks like he's still a handful."

Herring barked as if he'd taken offense.

"Oh, he's not such a bad boy," said Mrs. Maynard. "But it's a busy time of year for us at Merry's, and when we do find time to take Herring to the park it's hard to give him a good run."

"Why's that?" asked James.

Suddenly, Mrs. Maynard vanished from view. There was some noisy scuffling and a joyous bark from Herring before she appeared again. "He's not very good at coming when he's called," she admitted, answering James's question. "We've tried to get him trained, but it doesn't seem to make a difference."

"He's probably not being deliberately disobedient," said Mandy. "He might just have a short attention span."

"Well, he's certainly easily distracted," said Jenny Maynard. Then she gasped. "And his nose is *very* cold! Excuse me one moment, would you?"

Mandy swapped amused looks with James and Nadia as they listened to her struggle to get Herring away from the door. Finally, they heard a door shut, and the barking grew fainter.

Mrs. Maynard opened the door again and wiped

her forehead. "Sorry. I'm sure you didn't come here for
another display of bad behavior from Herring," she
said. "What can I do for you so early in the morning?"

"We came over last night, but you were out," Mandy
explained.

"Yes, Sam and I were being wined and dined by some
customers," said Mrs. Maynard. "What a drag. We had to
leave Herring with our neighbor, and the traffic was
awful."

Mandy smothered a smile. She got the impression
Jenny Maynard was as easily distracted as her dog!
"Sorry, Mrs. Maynard," she broke in gently, "but do you
have Barry Greenhalgh's address?"

She frowned, taken aback. "Possibly. Why?"

"We've got Alf, his girlfriend's rabbit," said James.

"She hopped into Mandy's bag by mistake," Nadia
added.

"Well, he and Rachel will be *thrilled* to hear that
piece of good news," said Jenny Maynard, beaming.
"And so am I! I felt simply dreadful when I heard the
poor little love was missing. Come inside for a moment,
and I'll see if I can find his number."

Mandy and her friends stepped into a cool, spacious
hall. The floor was tiled in black and white like a chess-
board, and several white squares held the trace of a

muddy paw print. A pathetic whining started up from behind a mahogany door.

"Ignore him, he's fine," said Mrs. Maynard, starting off down a passage. "I'll just go to the study."

"You know," said James slowly, "if Herring needs extra exercise, and Mr. and Mrs. Maynard are really busy at work . . ."

Mandy guessed what he was thinking. "Maybe we could walk him for them?"

"Are you sure that's a good idea?" Nadia frowned. "He's a bit wild."

"I don't think we saw him at his best yesterday," said Mandy.

"Besides, you must remember my Labrador, Blackie," said James. "I'm used to naughty dogs!"

"Well, I'm not!" Nadia grimaced. "Remember when you all came to visit last summer? Blackie chased a duck into the village pond and made everyone as muddy as he was."

James smiled at the memory. "Well, we'll keep Herring away from ponds just in case. How's that?"

Mrs. Maynard appeared at the end of the passageway, waving a piece of paper. "I have Barry's address, but he's not answering his phone."

"Maybe he's at Rachel's house," said Mandy. "Barry said she lived next door to him, I think."

"Do they live near here, Mrs. Maynard?" asked James.

"About half a mile or so," she said, offering Nadia the piece of paper.

Nadia read it quickly. "I know that street. My French tutor lives around there."

Mandy turned excitedly to her friends. "We've walked for a mile already. What's another half mile? We could leave a note for him!"

Nadia nodded, her dark eyes shining. "Or if they're back, we could even break the news in person!"

"And maybe," James began shyly, "we could take Herring with us?"

Jenny Maynard stared at him in surprise. "You? Take Herring?"

"We'd take good care of him," Mandy promised. "We just thought —"

"My dears, *please*!" Mrs. Maynard laughed. "The thought of you taking Herring for a long walk is *divine*!" She smiled at Mandy. "After yesterday, I have no doubt at all that he'll be in safe hands. I'll just get his leash." She turned and went back down the hall. "Promise you won't change your mind before I get back."

James gave Mandy and Nadia a thumbs-up. Herring started scratching at the door and whining more loudly.

"He knows something's going on," Nadia observed.

Mrs. Maynard came back with a retractable leash. Taking a deep breath, she opened the door a little way, blocking Herring's escape with her legs while she struggled to clip the leash onto his collar. When she'd succeeded, she stepped aside, and Herring charged into the hall, looking overjoyed to see so many visitors.

"Sit, boy!" Mandy said firmly.

Herring skidded to a stop and cocked his head to one side, wagging his tail at her expectantly. His red-brown frame was muscular, but possibly just a little on the tubby side, which wasn't surprising if he didn't get enough exercise. His eyes were a heart-melting brown, and his nose was black and shiny.

"He's all yours," said Jenny Maynard, passing the leash to James. "Good luck!"

"We'll bring him back by lunchtime," Mandy assured her.

Mrs. Maynard chuckled. "Is that a promise or a threat?"

As they made their way through the quiet streets, Mandy, James, and Nadia soon learned that Herring didn't just go for a walk. He went for a run, a meander, a circle-around-behind-you, and a sudden dash into people's front yards.

At one point, he started chasing his tail and ended up

with his leash wound tightly around a tree. "He makes Blackie look like a trained guide dog!" exclaimed James, struggling to sort out the tangle.

A few minutes later, Mandy was nearly yanked off her feet when the Irish setter tried dashing off to investigate someone walking on the other side of the road. Nadia grabbed hold of Mandy just in time to stop her from falling.

"Bad dog, Herring!" she scolded.

Herring barked and looked mournful for a couple of moments. But soon he was trotting along cheerily as if nothing had happened.

"He might have hurt himself if he'd run out into the road," said Mandy. "This dog really needs some good training."

"The trouble is, he's interested in just about everything and everyone," said Nadia. "And if you try to be strict with him, he thinks you're playing a game."

"Poor Herring," said James, taking the leash from Mandy. "There must be *some* way to keep you under control."

Soon they arrived at Barry Greenhalgh's street. They rang the bell at number 36, but no one was in.

"Rachel lives next door," Mandy mused. "But which way, left or right?"

"What do you think, Herring?" James joked.

Herring pulled toward the left.

"We'll take your advice," said Mandy, laughing.

As it turned out, he was exactly right. Rachel answered the door, her frizzy red hair standing on end and her eyes slightly puffy. She looked blankly at them for a few moments before she recognized James — and Herring.

"Hello," she said. "What's this? Why have you brought that crazy hound here?"

"Never mind," Mandy blurted out. "Fantastic news! We've found Alf! She's safe."

"What?" Rachel stared at them in shock. "You're not joking, are you?"

Mandy shook her head. "She snuck into my backpack in all the mayhem yesterday, and I accidentally took her back to Nadia's house."

Barry appeared behind Rachel. "Hello, kids," he called. "What's all this about good news?"

"It's the best!" cried Rachel, hugging him. "Oh, I can't believe it! Alf's safe!"

Mandy, James, and Nadia told them the whole story. Bored, Herring lay down at Mandy's feet and licked at her ankle through her sock.

"Unbelievable," said a beaming Barry. "But I'm afraid a friend of mine has borrowed my car to move today. I won't get it back till this afternoon. Is it all right if we drive over to pick up Alf then?"

"No problem," said Nadia, giving him the address. "She's in Pixie's run, eating grass. She can stay there till you pick her up."

"Are you sure?" Rachel asked anxiously. "You've already been so kind, looking after Alf overnight."

"It's been fun," said Mandy. "Anyway, you'll be giving us a chance to say good-bye to her."

"And I promise we won't take Herring anywhere near her!" James added. "We're dropping him off on the way home."

"All sorts of animal traffic going this way and that, isn't there?" Barry laughed. "Well, thanks, kids. You've been great. Oh, before you go . . ." He pulled out a pen and a scrap of paper and scrawled on the back of it. "Here's Rachel's number if anything happens in the meantime." He gave the note to Mandy, who put it in her pocket. "We'll see you later."

Barry and Rachel disappeared back inside the house, and James tugged on Herring's leash. He was back on his paws in an instant and leading them back along the street.

Nadia sighed happily. "I'm so glad we came over in person."

"Me, too," said Mandy. "But now I can't wait to get back so we can say a long good-bye to Alf."

"I don't think Herring can wait to get back home,

either," said James, panting, as the dog shot off down the road, dragging him along.

Mandy rolled her eyes. "Come on," she said to Nadia. "We'd better catch up to them!"

By the time she arrived back at the Maynards' house, Mandy was hot and red in the face, with very sore feet. James and Nadia looked worn out, too. Even Herring looked a little less lively.

"That was a good, long walk," said Jenny Maynard, who answered the door when they knocked. Herring leaped up to greet her, but once she'd ruffled his ears, he sprawled flat out on the cool floor, panting. "You seem to have taken a little of the bounce out of him," she added.

"Good," James said wearily. "Because he's taken a *lot* of the bounce out of us!"

"How about some homemade lemonade and cookies to put some of it back?" asked Mrs. Maynard.

"Sounds great!" said Mandy, smiling.

Soon they were munching rich, buttery cookies in the Maynards' kitchen. Sam Maynard, a lean, unassuming man with graying hair and a beard, served them the lemonade before retiring to his study.

"Working on a Sunday," Jenny Maynard tutted. "He never stops. That's why you're eating cookies," she added. "I refuse to have any chocolate in the house. Otherwise we'd never get away from it."

"Shame," said James without thinking. "We missed out on the free samples yesterday. I thought you might have a few lying around here!"

"Aha!" cried Mrs. Maynard. "So you had an ulterior motive for walking Herring, eh?"

"Oh, no," James protested, turning bright red. "In fact, we'd really like to walk him again later this week, if that's OK."

"I have an English lesson tomorrow afternoon," said Nadia. "If you and Mandy wanted something to do then . . ."

"Well, if you haven't been put out, that's fine with me," said Jenny Maynard, smiling. "But just so you don't wear yourselves out completely, I'd better give you a ride back home."

"You're a lifesaver," said Mandy through a mouthful of crumbs. "I feel like we've walked all around York a dozen times."

Mrs. Maynard took them home in her Jeep. The seats were covered with rust-colored hairs, and Mandy could easily imagine Herring bouncing all over them. She was already looking forward to seeing the lively dog again.

"See you two tomorrow!" called Jenny Maynard as she drove away.

"Is it only noon?" groaned James, checking his watch. "I'm ready for bed already!"

Mandy nudged him in the ribs. "You wouldn't want to miss our last chance to play with Alf, would you?"

"Well, *I'm* going to see how Pixie is," Nadia announced, unlatching the gate that led to the backyard.

Mandy and James followed her to the hutch, which sat squarely in the shade of the elder. But when they lifted up the lid, the hutch was empty.

"Where's Pixie?" cried Nadia, staring around in panic.

"Relax," said Aunt Mina, appearing through the patio doors dressed in shorts and a T-shirt. "It's such a lovely day that I put him outside with Alf."

"What?" Nadia frowned at her mom. "Have you checked to see that they're all right?"

"They seem very fond of each other," said Aunt Mina. "Why not see for yourself?"

Mandy and James went over to the run and knelt down on the grass. Alf and Pixie were snuggled up side by side in the shady part, a fluffy heap of dark blue and caramel-colored fur.

"They're like best friends," Mandy murmured.

"Yes, well," said Nadia, "I still don't think Mom should have interfered. Pixie is *my* rabbit!"

James rolled his eyes at Mandy behind Nadia's back.

"Well, look on the bright side. Now we know we can play with both of them together."

They spent the whole afternoon in the spring sunshine with the two bunnies. Alf had an endearing habit. Whenever you put her somewhere else in the yard, she would race back to the run and wait to be let inside.

"Some pets try to escape their pens," Mandy said, laughing. "Not Alf!"

"I guess she's had enough of great escapes," James joked.

But Pixie was a lot less lively and didn't seem interested in playing. He was content just to sit on Nadia's lap, letting her stroke his long floppy ears.

At half-past four, Barry and Rachel arrived to take Alf home. Rachel raced across the yard to see her beloved rabbit.

"Time to say good-bye, guys," Mandy told the two rabbits.

"There you are, Alfie!" cried Rachel. "And in such a lovely run, too!"

Nadia shrugged and smiled, then lifted the run so Rachel could pick up her pet. Pixie sat and watched quite calmly. But once Alf had been lifted out, the lop-eared rabbit hopped out from under the shady strip and watched his friend leave with a mournful look in his eyes.

"You'll see Alf again at the judging on Wednesday," Nadia promised him.

"We haven't decided if we're going yet," Rachel admitted. "Now that I have Alf back, I'm not sure I want to let her out of my sight again."

"I know how you must feel," said Mandy, "but I hope we see you there, anyway."

After they'd waved good-bye to Barry, Rachel, and Alf, they all collapsed onto the lawn again.

"What a day!" Mandy puffed. "I'm beat!"

"How about some orange Popsicles and a cool drink to revive you?" suggested Aunt Mina. She smiled. "That is, if you're quite sure no one *else* is coming to visit."

"Thanks, Mom," said Nadia. "That'll keep us going while we lavish all our care and attention on Pixie!"

But it seemed as if Pixie wanted to be left alone now that Alf had gone. He kept trying to hop away from Nadia when she petted him. He didn't even show much interest in any of the delicious weeds that Mandy found.

"He's still in a funny mood," said Nadia, sipping her drink. "I wish you could tell me what's on your mind, little one, so I could try to make things better."

James sucked at the last of his Popsicle. "He might be feeling a bit unsettled," he suggested. "Just as he started getting to know Alf, she's gone again."

"You're probably right," Nadia agreed.

Mandy crouched in front of Pixie to offer him another weed. The rabbit ignored it. Perhaps it was the light, but his eyes looked just a little duller than they had that morning.

"What are you looking at, Mandy?" Nadia asked.

"Oh — nothing," Mandy said quickly. "I was just thinking that Pixie's obviously missing Alf, that's all."

She looked at the little bunny sitting quietly on the grass and crossed her fingers that nothing else was wrong.

Six

Mandy awoke the next morning to find she was alone in Nadia's bedroom. It was just after eight o'clock, and the sun was warm and orange through the curtains. Rubbing her eyes, she got out of bed and padded over to the window. Aunt Mina was doing some gardening by the old city wall, and directly below she saw Nadia busy at Pixie's hutch.

Throwing on some clothes, she went out onto the landing. James was just coming out of his own room in his pajamas. He smothered a large yawn when he saw Mandy.

"That was a good sleep," he said. "That double bed is so soft I could stay in it forever."

"The cot's a bit lumpy," Mandy commented, "but I was so tired I think I could have slept on the kitchen floor. Come on, Nadia's outside with Pixie."

"It's just like her to be up early," said James.

"She's probably worried about him." Mandy frowned. "And so am I."

Nadia looked up as they came onto the patio. She was cradling Pixie in the crook of her elbow. "Hi," she said without much enthusiasm.

"Is Pixie still under the weather?" Mandy asked. The little rabbit's ears seemed extra droopy, and his dark eyes still looked a little dull.

"He hasn't eaten much of last night's dinner," Nadia told her. "But I think he looks a bit brighter than he did yesterday."

Mandy paused. "Do you want me to take a look at him?"

"I just made him comfy on my arm." Nadia gave her an impatient look. "Please, Mandy, I know you mean well, but I *do* know how to look after him, OK?"

Mandy blushed. "Sorry, I didn't mean to seem pushy."

"I bet Pixie's still pining for Alf," said James, changing the subject. "Animals can be deeply affected by friends leaving. Hey, Mandy, remember Walter Pickard's cat, Tom?"

She nodded. "How could I forget?" When Tom's companion, Scraps, had to be put to sleep following a kidney infection, Tom nearly pined away with sadness. Luckily, a stray cat became an excellent new friend for him, and Tom made a full recovery.

But Tom and Scraps had been together for years. Alf and Pixie had barely known each other for a day. There were no obvious signs that anything was actually wrong with Pixie, but Mandy knew that rabbits got sick very swiftly.

"Well, I'm sure Pixie's not going to be as bad as Walter Whoever's cat," said Nadia. "He'll be fine. Now, I'd better get ready for my English lesson." She gave Mandy and James a shrewd look. "And *you'd* better get ready to walk Herring. You did tell Mrs. Maynard you would!"

With that, she breezed back indoors.

"She just doesn't want us playing with Pixie while she's gone." Mandy sighed. "Still, I suppose there's nothing to worry about just yet."

"We'll keep an eye on Pixie when we get back," James assured her. "Even if we have to do it in secret, when Nadia's not looking."

* * *

Mandy's mood brightened as she walked with James to Mrs. Maynard's house. The sky was an almost perfect blue, with only a few fluffy scraps of white cloud. For a while they walked along the top of the city wall, enjoying the view into other people's yards.

As they passed a particularly large garden, Mandy heard a voice she recognized, high-pitched and a little petulant.

James had heard the voice, too. "That's Angelica Angell," he whispered, "the girl with Princess Powderpuff."

They peered down into the yard and saw Angelica sitting on a large pink beanbag with her beloved rabbit on her lap. Three girls sat on the grass looking up at her, seeming to hang on her every word.

"Anyway," Angelica was saying, "that silly man next door had the nerve to call my precious puff ball a *rodent*!" She scrunched up her nose. The other girls did the same, but they seemed a little puzzled. "He thought *all* rabbits were rodents, you see."

"So did I!" James admitted quietly.

"I'm not sure I've ever really thought about it," said Mandy, intrigued.

"They're actually *lagomorphs*, I told him," said Angelica. "The breeder told Mommy when we got my perfect

princess. It means 'formed like a hare.' Nasty old rats are rodents — rabbits aren't the same thing at all. They have different teeth and everything."

"You're so smart, Angelica," said one of the girls admiringly.

James grimaced. "I'll be sick if I hear any more of this."

Mandy agreed. "Yes, I think we've learned enough for one day. Come on, let's leave them to it."

Now that they knew where they were going, the journey to the Maynards' seemed to take less time. Mrs. Maynard answered the door, and this time, as she put Herring on his retractable leash, she directed them to a nearby park.

"Lots of room for him to cause chaos in," she said, beaming and handing the leash to James.

"Are we allowed to let him run free?" Mandy asked.

"If you're feeling brave!" Mrs. Maynard laughed.

"We'll play it by ear," Mandy told her. "Thanks."

When they reached the park, Herring jumped up at James and Mandy, barking with excitement. The tempting expanse of grass was dotted with trees and tailored shrubbery. Some boys and girls were playing a football game using oak trees as goalposts. People walked their dogs, pushed children in strollers, or simply lay down in the sunshine with books or newspapers.

Herring strained at the leash. "He knows this is a place where he can have some fun," said James. "Shall we let him off?"

Mandy shook her head. "Let's fix his leash to the longest setting first."

James pressed the button on the handle, and the red cord played out as Herring trotted away. When it had reached its limit, it gently jerked him back. Herring stared back mournfully at James.

"Here, boy!" Mandy called. "Herring!" She bent over and patted her knees. "Come, Herring. Come here."

Herring cocked his head to one side and took a few steps toward her. But then a girl walked past with an ice cream cone, and he started to follow her instead.

"No, Herring!" said Mandy. "Here!"

Herring turned back to look at her and James. After a few moments, he trotted over to them and looked adoringly up at Mandy.

"Good boy," she said, patting him behind the ears. "We just need to make sure you're not so distracted, don't we?"

But even as she spoke, a voice floated across the park. "Jerry! Here boy!" Mandy looked up to see, some distance away, an old man squinting into the sunlight as he looked around. "Jerry? Where are you, boy?"

Herring barked and raced off in the man's direction. Caught by surprise, James let out a yelp as the handle of the leash was snatched from his hand. The setter was a rusty blur against the bright green grass as he tore up to the old man.

"Oh, no!" James wailed.

"It's not your fault." Mandy put a reassuring hand on his arm before jogging off after the disappearing dog. "He misheard 'Jerry' for 'Herring,' that's all."

"That dog needs brain surgery," James said ruefully, running after her. "And so do I for not keeping a tighter grip on his leash!"

By the time they caught up with Herring he was sitting expectantly beside the bewildered old man.

"Is this one with you?" he asked as they arrived. "I wish my Jerry came as quickly." He pointed to a wide-eyed pug who was trotting toward them.

Mandy smiled. "I wish Herring had legs as tiny as your pug. We'd catch up with him quicker."

James picked up the handle of the leash and retracted the extendable cord. Herring let out a yelp of protest. He was watching the pug approach, his tail wagging.

"Herring!" Mandy commanded. "Heel, boy! Come on, Herring."

But Jerry gave a high-pitched yip, and all of Herring's

attention was taken once again. He barked cheerily and tried to bowl over to the little dog. But this time James hung on to the leash.

"Herring's bright, but so easily distracted," Mandy mused. "We need to find a way to get his attention — and keep it."

They paused to let a young father with a stroller cross in front of them. The toddler threw out her rattle, which landed in the grass with a noisy shake. Instantly, Herring was alert, watching closely as Mandy retrieved the rattle and handed it back to the little girl.

"Mandy, that's it!" cried James. "Maybe he could learn to recognize a sound!"

Mandy frowned. "You mean we should shake a rattle when we call him?"

"Not an ordinary rattle." He grinned at her. "But a little box of treats would rattle if it was shaken, wouldn't it?"

"Of course!" Mandy smiled back at him. "When we want him to do something, we shake the box of treats! If he thinks he's going to get a one, we'll certainly have his attention. That's brilliant, James! We'll tell Mrs. Maynard and put together Herring's very own treat box!"

They walked and ran around with Herring for some time, keeping him firmly on the leash. Then, while James rested beside the contented setter, Mandy picked some dandelion leaves.

"Hopefully, these will cheer Pixie up," she said, stuffing her pockets full of the deep green jagged leaves as they left the park and headed back to the Maynards' house. She hadn't forgotten how miserable the lop-eared rabbit had looked that morning, and she still had a nagging feeling that there might be a bigger problem than Alf's departure.

"A box of treats! What an great idea!" declared Jenny Maynard, looking thoughtfully at her panting dog. "Well, we can soon test James's theory. I've got plenty of Tupperware containers in the kitchen. And we can easily cut up some strips of jerky and add a few dog biscuits."

After Mrs. Maynard found a container, Mandy and James set to work cutting up chews and jerky. Herring sniffed around them for a while, then drank noisily from his water dish. As he raised his head he saw something in the yard. A moment later the water dish was sent flying as Herring launched himself over to the door, barking furiously.

"Oh, no, he's spotted a squirrel," Mrs. Maynard called over the noise.

James picked up the container of treats, popped the lid on it, and gave it a sudden shake.

Herring stopped barking and pricked his ears.

"Look, it works!" cried Mandy.

"Sit, Herring," said James in his firmest voice, the one he used on Blackie. He shook the treat box again. "Sit, boy. Sit!"

Herring did as he was told and sat beside the back door.

"Well, goodness me!" exclaimed Mrs. Maynard.

James peeled open the plastic lid and threw the setter a doggy treat. Herring munched it happily and then got up and walked away.

"No, Herring," called James. "Stay." He shook the treat box, but Herring ignored it.

"Oh, dear," Mrs. Maynard said, and sighed.

"Herring!" Mandy commanded. At her signal, James gave the treat box another vigorous shake. "Here, boy."

Herring paused, then trotted back.

"He's starting to get the idea!" cried Mrs. Maynard. She patted James and Mandy heartily on the back. "Good job, you two. How would you like a guided tour of the chocolate factory tomorrow, as a thank-you from Herring and me?"

"Wow!" said Mandy. "That would be amazing!"

"Absolutely!" declared James.

"Your friend Nadia can come, too, if she likes," Mrs. Maynard went on. "I'll pick you up at nine-thirty sharp. You just have to promise to stay close to me and not to touch anything."

"Don't worry, we'll behave," said Mandy. She winked at James. "Even without a treat box!"

Mrs. Maynard gave Mandy and James a ride back to Aunt Mina's house. Nadia greeted them from the yard, where she was grooming Pixie. A long, fat carrot sat in front of the little rabbit.

"Hi, Nadia," Mandy said. "Is Pixie feeling better?"

"I think a little bit," said Nadia. "He doesn't mind me petting his back. And look, he's eating."

She held up the carrot. James swapped a dubious glance with Mandy. It had barely been scratched.

"Well, I brought him some dandelion leaves from the park," Mandy said. "Maybe he'd like some of them, too."

"Oh, yes, he's always loved dandelion leaves," said Nadia.

While James told Nadia all about Herring's antics and his brainstorm about the treat box, Mandy watched Pixie hop forward to inspect her offering. His nose twitched, and he pressed his toffee-colored head into the leaves. Mandy held her breath, willing him to start eating, but then the little rabbit seemed to lose interest and hopped back to Nadia.

"Never mind," said James. "We can leave them in his hutch. He'll probably eat them later."

"Of course he will," said Nadia, scooping him up in both

hands. "He's just feeling shy. I'll pop him back in his hutch for now, and we can go inside. Mom let me choose some videos after my class. We can watch them with pizza."

"Sounds great," replied Mandy.

But James looked slightly worried. "They're not all about how to do folk dancing, are they?"

Nadia laughed. "Only the first three," she joked.

They spent the rest of the day watching the videos, which were action-packed blockbusters, much to James's relief. But though Mandy tried hard to concentrate on the twists and turns of the plot, she couldn't help thinking of Pixie and his mysterious loss of appetite. Could it really just be due to missing Alf?

As the end credits rolled on the second movie, Mandy struggled up from her comfy armchair. "Is it OK if I call home, Mrs. Hunter?" she asked. "I'd like to see how the animals in the residential unit are doing."

"Help yourself, it's in the hall," said Aunt Mina, smiling.

"Say hi to your mom and dad for me," James called through a mouthful of pizza crust.

Mandy was glad the noise of the TV meant that no one in the living room would overhear her conversation. She had decided to ask her parents for advice on Pixie, just to put her mind at rest, but she knew if Nadia found out, she would think Mandy was accusing her of not looking after Pixie properly.

Mandy dialed the number. To her surprise, her grandmother answered.

"I wasn't expecting you to be there!" Mandy said. "How are things? Is everything all right?"

"Mandy!" Gran cried. "How lovely to hear from you. Yes, everything's fine. Your mom and dad have gone out to dinner with some friends, so your grandpa and I are babysitting the animals."

"Will they be out late?" Mandy wondered.

"I think so." Gran paused. "Can I take a message for them?"

"No, it doesn't matter," Mandy said quickly. Nadia had just opened the door and breezed past with a smile, carrying the dirty plates to the kitchen. "James and I are having a great time."

"Oh, I'm pleased," said Gran. "Well, we'll pass that on to them. Perhaps you could call again tomorrow."

"Yes, I'll do that," said Mandy. "Thanks, Gran. Bye!" She put down the phone with a sigh.

Nadia came back into the hallway. "Were they out?" she asked. "Bad luck. Hey, don't look so down. The next video will take your mind off it."

But Mandy's mind wasn't on her parents. It was on Pixie, outside in his luxurious hutch. She knew Nadia had convinced herself that nothing was wrong with her rabbit — but was she right?

Seven

Mandy was woken the next morning by James's voice floating up from downstairs. It sounded like he was on the phone. Her first thought was that her mom and dad had called back and that James must have answered. What if he said something about Pixie, and Nadia overheard?

Mandy jumped up from her cot. The other bed was empty. Scrambling over to the window, she saw Aunt Mina weeding again in the yard. But there was no sign of Nadia.

Throwing on her robe, she ran downstairs, signaling

frantically at James, who looked at her with his eyebrows raised.

"Uh, hold on a minute," he said into the phone. "Mandy, what's up?"

"Is that my mom and dad?" she hissed.

James frowned. "No, it's Blackie's kennel. I dreamed about him last night and wanted to check that he was OK. Aunt Mina said I could."

"Sorry, James," said Mandy, slumping down onto the bottom stair in relief. Over the sound of his talking on the phone, she heard a shower running upstairs. Nadia must be in the bathroom.

Mandy knew she was being silly, carrying on like this. If Pixie really was ill, then she needed to make Nadia take the rabbit to her own vet.

"Is Blackie all right?" she asked as James put down the phone.

"He's doing really well." James grinned. "Apart from wriggling out of his kennel to have a run around the yard, and eating another dog's dinner, he's been good as gold!"

"Glad to hear he's up to his old tricks," Mandy said fondly.

James nodded. "I wonder if Herring has learned any new tricks with his treat box?"

"Hey, what time is it?" asked Mandy.

James checked his watch. "After nine."

"Mrs. Maynard's coming to pick us up at half past!" Mandy realized. She ran back up the stairs. "We'd better get ready. I want to check on Pixie before we go."

Nadia came out of the bathroom wrapped in a towel. "I'll just get dressed and fix us some breakfast," she offered, disappearing into her bedroom. "See you in the kitchen."

Mandy showered and dressed in record time, then joined James and Nadia downstairs. The room was filled with delicious smells. Nadia was bending over a sizzling frying pan, and James had just cleared his plate with a satisfied expression.

"Wow, I didn't expect pancakes for breakfast!" said Mandy.

"We've run out of cornflakes," said Nadia, smiling over her shoulder. "Although these aren't just pancakes. They're *clătite*."

Mandy tried repeating the word herself. "Cla-tee-tay?"

"That's right," Nadia told her. "A Romanian crêpe. They're lighter and thinner than normal pancakes. It's one of Mom's old recipes — about the only one I like!"

"We've already eaten ours. I can't remember how to pronounce them, but they taste great," James said happily. He held up a little glass jar from the table. "You have them with homemade grape jam."

"1 hope you've saved some for Mandy," Nadia warned, serving a perfect pancake onto Mandy's plate.

"Thanks, Nadia," said Mandy, helping herself to the last dollop of jam. "You're a great cook, just like your mom!"

Nadia swiftly washed the pan and checked her watch. "Nine-thirty," she said. "Just enough time to see Pixie before we go."

Mandy swallowed the last mouthful of her *clătite* and followed James and Nadia into the living room.

"Hi, Mom!" said Nadia, giving her mother a hug. "You were up early."

"The yard doesn't look after itself," she said, wiping her hand across her forehead. "Are you ready to go? Jenny Maynard should be here any minute now."

As she spoke, the doorbell rang.

"Can you get the door, Mom?" asked Nadia. "We want to say good-bye to Pixie."

Quickly, they went to the patio. Nadia lifted up the lid of the hutch.

"Oh, *look*!" she squealed. "Those dandelion leaves you gave her. They're all gone!"

Mandy felt an enormous wave of relief wash over her. "You're right, she's eaten all of them."

"Good Pixie," beamed James. "I'm glad Alf hasn't broken his heart by moving out!"

Pixie was curled up beneath a tangle of straw. Nadia stroked one of his long fluffy ears, and he gave a quiet squeak.

"Come on, kids!" called Aunt Mina. "Mrs. Maynard is waiting in her car for you."

"We'd better go," said Nadia, carefully closing the lid of the hutch. "But we'll be back to give you lots of cuddles later, Pixie."

"Definitely," said Mandy. She felt like a huge weight had been lifted off her shoulders. No need to worry about Pixie. No need to convince Nadia she should call the vet. Now she could relax and enjoy the tour of the chocolate factory — and the rest of the vacation!

"So this is it," said Mandy as she, James, and Nadia stood looking out over the noisy factory floor. The large room was filled with thrumming machines, steaming vats, and snaking pipework. The smell of chocolate was almost overpowering.

"Yes, this is where most of our chocolate is made," said Mrs. Maynard, raising her voice above the noise.

Mandy noticed that all the workers wore white overalls, gloves, and clear plastic shower caps over their hair. "What are they for?"

"We have to keep the place hygienic," said Mrs. Maynard, producing a bundle of gloves and caps. "We don't want foreign material in the chocolate." Once they'd put on the gear, their guide led them forward.

"We start by roasting and blending the cocoa beans together into a special mix," Jenny Maynard explained. "We use several different types, and it's a big secret because the combination of different beans is what gives Merry's its special taste."

"Blending is what coffee makers do with coffee beans, isn't it?" Nadia asked.

"That's right." Mrs. Maynard nodded. "Once we've taken the nibs from the beans — the edible part inside the shell — we grind them to make chocolate liquor." James opened his mouth to speak, but she stopped him with a raised hand. "And no, it's not that sort of liquor. It's just a thick liquid — pure unsweetened chocolate."

"Pure chocolate," James said dreamily. "I wasn't expecting my stomach to start rumbling so soon after breakfast."

"It's very bitter," Jenny Maynard warned him. "To make it pleasant to eat we have to add sugar, milk, and flavorings, following a special traditional Merry's recipe."

"Does that happen in that big machine there?" asked Mandy, gesturing to the large, shuddering contraption beside them.

"No, that's the hydraulic press where we squeeze the fat out of the chocolate liquor to get cocoa butter," explained Mrs. Maynard. "We use that to make our white chocolate, among other things."

"What about that row of machines over there?" James pointed to a row of silver-gray boxes that looked like an oven crossed with a washing machine.

"That's where the conching takes place," said Mrs. Maynard. "Conching is when we massage the chocolate, smooth it out, and blend all the ingredients together. We leave it in there for almost a day and a half before it's ready."

Mandy frowned. "I thought a conch was a sort of shell."

"It is," their guide confirmed. "The process is called 'conching' because in the days when chocolate was made entirely by hand, the device they used looked like a conch."

"And is the chocolate ready then?" asked Nadia.

"Good gracious, no," replied Mrs. Maynard. "The conched chocolate glugs down those pipes into another big machine to be slowly heated and then cooled. That's called 'tempering.' If we didn't do that, the chocolate wouldn't harden properly and would look like a mess."

"It must have taken people ages before machines did all the work," said James, clearly impressed.

"Some of our chocolate is still homemade," said Mrs. Maynard. "Our top-of-the-line truffles, for instance. Come on, I'll show you."

She led the way through a sparkling clean corridor to a quieter, older part of the factory. As they passed through a reception area, Mandy's jaw dropped.

"Look at that!" she said, and gasped. "It's a miniature model of the street from *Parson's Close* — made entirely of chocolate!"

"That's right," Mrs. Maynard said proudly. "They wanted it made to mark the one-thousandth episode. Do you watch the show?"

"It's my favorite soap," said Mandy. "My friend's mother is in it."

"Cool!" declared Nadia. "Which one?"

"That's her, there!" said James excitedly, staring at a photo on the reception wall. "Miranda Collins!" The glamorous star was pictured smiling beside the chocolate model.

"I can't wait to tell Susan that her mom's on the wall at Merry's," said Mandy.

Mrs. Maynard led them through to a smaller workplace, teeming with workers. There were just as many machines in here, but most of them were far smaller. Over at a table set apart from the organized mayhem of the chocolate making, Mandy recognized Barry Greenhalgh and Sam Maynard, dressed in matching white lab coats with plastic caps on their heads.

"Hey, you guys," said Barry. "Getting the guided tour, are you?"

"Yes," said Nadia, "it's amazing!"

"How's Alf?" asked Mandy.

"Happy as can be." Barry smiled.

"So Rachel will be bringing her for Wednesday's judging?" asked Mandy.

Barry nodded. "Looks like it."

"Never mind the rabbits," said Sam Maynard. "You've come just in time to help me out. I'm trying to decide on a new flavor of chocolate truffle. Barry's gathered a whole bunch of ingredients together, but I'm feeling a little stumped."

Mandy scanned the ingredients on the table. There were cherries, sugared almonds, sticky toffee, chunky nougat, creamy-looking fondants in at least twelve different colors. . . . "I'm not surprised you're stumped," she said. "What a choice!"

James stepped forward with a serious look on his face.

"Here's a bit of chocolate," said Barry, passing him a little dark square. "Load it up with whatever you like."

James licked his lips and got busy. "I think we'll have a bit of this, and this." He spooned a small piece of soft fudge onto the chocolate and then, after some agonizing, added a dollop of strawberry fondant. "Now for the finishing touch." He added a few white chocolate shavings and presented it to Sam Maynard, who took it from him.

"An intriguing choice, young man," he said. "I'm not sure what it will taste like, but . . ."

He winked at Mandy and Nadia and popped it in his mouth. He started to chew, and as Mandy watched, a pleased smile spread slowly over his face.

"Not bad at all!" he said. "Distinctive flavor, but I think it would work better with milk chocolate than dark. Make up some samples, would you, Barry? We'll decorate it with white chocolate stripes, I think."

James looked astonished. "You mean you'll make some of my chocolates? For real?"

"We'll certainly test them further, son," said Mr. Maynard. "I'm not promising they'll make it into production, but we'll see what our tasters think."

"That's really cool, James!" said Nadia.

"Yeah, well done," Mandy added, proudly putting an arm around his shoulders.

James grinned at them both. "This is just the best Easter vacation ever!"

When Mrs. Maynard dropped them at home in time for lunch, weighed down with chocolate samples, Mandy, Nadia, and James bustled into the house wearing grins from ear to ear.

Aunt Mina was in the kitchen, rinsing some vegetables under the tap. "Hello, everyone," she called. "You had fun?"

"Loads of fun!" said James. "I'm a chocolate maker in training!"

"And by the time we've finished eating all these free

goodies, we'll all be expert chocolate tasters," joked Nadia.

"Well, please wait until after lunch," said Aunt Mina.

Mandy noticed a pile of groundsel on the drain board. "Looks like Pixie's going to have hers, too!"

Aunt Mina turned with a slightly worried expression. "I hope so. She didn't seem to eat any of her dinner last night. I had to throw away a big pile of dandelion leaves first thing this morning. They were all withered."

Mandy felt her stomach twist with worry. "You threw the leaves away?"

Nadia was standing as pale and still as a statue. "But when they weren't there this morning, we thought Pixie had eaten them!"

"No, he hadn't touched them," Aunt Mina said sadly. "I meant to tell you, but then Mrs. Maynard arrived and I didn't want to spoil your trip to the factory." She sighed. "I gave Pixie some groundsel after you'd gone, but he hasn't touched that, either. I was just about to give him this fresh bunch."

"Oh, Pixie," said Nadia, her eyes welling with tears as she ran from the room. Mandy and James rushed after her.

When they reached the patio, Nadia was standing over the hutch with its lid raised. "He looks so sad," she murmured, tears streaking her face. "Oh, Pixie, what's happened?"

Mandy peered into the hutch and was shocked to see the difference in Pixie even since yesterday. Because he had hidden in the straw, none of them had noticed this morning, but he looked noticeably thinner now that he had moved out of his cozy nest. His eyes, so dark and clear when Mandy had first met him, were dull and half closed. Nadia reached in to stroke his ears, but he squeaked loudly, and she snatched back her hand.

"I'm sorry, Nadia, but I think Pixie should see a vet right away," said Mandy.

"No," said Nadia, closing the lid of the hutch. "A vet might put him to sleep!"

Mandy forced herself to keep calm. "A vet might be able to help Pixie, to tell us what's wrong with him. This could be serious."

"It's not fair," Nadia wailed, close to tears. "I don't want Pixie to be sick."

"Look, why don't I call my mom and dad for some advice?" Mandy suggested. Nadia nodded, ashen faced. There was nothing grown-up and aloof about her now. She looked small and scared, like a little girl.

Mandy quickly asked permission to use the phone, then dialed Animal Ark.

"Emily Hope," her mom answered.

"Oh, Mom!" Mandy said. "I'm so glad you're there!"

"Mandy! Is everything OK?"

"No," said Mandy. "I think Nadia's rabbit could be sick."

"What are the symptoms?" Emily Hope asked calmly.

Mandy described Pixie's loss of appetite and depression and the dull look in his eyes. "First, we thought Pixie was just missing Alf," she added.

"Alf?"

"Another rabbit — it's a long story," said Mandy. "Alf ended up sharing a hutch and a run with Pixie for a day and a night."

"Rabbits don't usually form such deep attachments, especially not in forty-eight hours," said Dr. Emily. "But they can catch diseases very quickly. Alf wasn't a wild rabbit, was he?"

"She," Mandy corrected. "No, she was a sweet little dark blue dwarf, and very well looked after."

"Even so, Mandy, you know how easily cross infection can occur between animals. You might not have been able to tell there was something wrong with Alf in such a short time."

"Well, it's not myxomatosis," Mandy said firmly. "Pixie's eyes have lost their shine, but there's no swelling or discharge."

"That's not the only contagious rabbit infection, I'm afraid." Dr. Emily paused. "Only yesterday we had to deal with a case of VHD."

"VHD?" Mandy echoed. "I've heard of it, but —"

"It stands for viral hemorrhagic disease. It's a fairly new disease. The first outbreak in our area was reported in 1992. It's deadly, and only rabbits can catch it. The virus makes them bleed to death inside."

Mandy bit her lip. "Is that what happened yesterday? The rabbit died?"

"Not just one rabbit, I'm afraid. In a case of VHD, all rabbits on the premises have to be destroyed. Even if they seem healthy, they can pass the disease on." Dr. Emily sighed. "This breeder had twenty-four, and none of them were vaccinated for VHD. Such a waste . . ."

Mandy tried to swallow the lump rising in her throat. "But — but there has to be a cure!"

"No one's found one yet," Dr. Emily admitted. "Only a vaccination can prevent it. Once a rabbit's caught the disease, it'll be dead within a few days."

Mandy said nothing, willing herself not to break down in tears.

"I'm so sorry to upset you, honey," said Dr. Emily. "Pixie may have had her VHD injection, and it might very well be something else altogether. The case has been preying on my mind a bit, that's all." Mandy heard a commotion of barking in the background. "Look, I'd better go, Mandy. But I'd get Pixie to a vet immediately. With symptoms like that you can't afford to wait around. Be brave, sweetheart. Bye-bye."

"Bye, Mom," whispered Mandy.

Nadia appeared in the living room doorway, with James just behind her.

"Well?" Nadia asked in a small voice.

"Has Pixie been inoculated for VHD?" Mandy demanded, feeling sick.

"VHD?" Nadia looked at her blankly. "No. No, I'm sure he hasn't."

"Why?" said James, standing just behind Nadia. "What's VHD?"

"Nadia, I — " Mandy wiped her eyes on her sleeve. "I think I may have some bad news."

Eight

"No!" Nadia shouted as Mandy started to explain about VHD. "I don't believe it! Pixie can't die just like that."

"It's only a possibility," Mandy said helplessly. "But we need to know. We need to get Pixie to a vet *now*."

"I won't let Pixie die," Nadia insisted. "I won't!"

Aunt Mina came rushing into the hallway, her face full of concern. "Hey, what's all this? Nadia?"

"Oh, Mom," wailed Nadia, and threw herself into her mother's arms. "Mandy's mom says Pixie's got some horrible deadly disease called VHD!"

"She's not certain," Mandy said. "Obviously, she

102

hasn't seen Pixie, but I described the symptoms over the phone."

"If this VHD is so deadly, why haven't we heard of it?" asked Aunt Mina, stroking Nadia's hair. "We took out a lot of books from the library, but I read nothing about this."

"If the books were written before 1992, the authors wouldn't have heard of it," Mandy explained. "That's when the first outbreak occurred."

"I see," said Aunt Mina. "Then we must take Pixie to the vet at once."

"But how would Pixie have caught it?" asked James.

"It's spread by other rabbits," Mandy told him. "It may have been Alf, or one of the other rabbits at the show."

"I bet it was Alf," hissed Nadia. "I said I didn't want her put in with Pixie, but no one listened!"

"But Barry didn't say there was anything wrong with Alf when we saw him this morning," James pointed out.

"So? He might not know his rabbit as well as I know Pixie." Nadia pulled away from her mother and stormed over to Mandy and James. "You made me put Alf in Pixie's hutch!" she cried. "And you put them together in Pixie's run, Mom! It's your fault, all of you!"

Aunt Mina looked close to tears, herself, as she reached out to her daughter. "That's not fair, Nadia."

"It is!" Nadia slapped her mom's hands away and

stormed up the stairs in tears. "If Pixie dies, it's your fault!"

She slammed her bedroom door. A shocked, uncomfortable silence fell on the house.

"I'm sorry for that outburst," Aunt Mina said quietly. "Nadia tends to act so much older than she is. It's her way of coping, I think — with having skipped a year in school and with all her extra classes. She convinces herself that she is all grown up, and she bottles up a lot of feelings. It is hard for her sometimes, I think."

"I can imagine," Mandy said with feeling.

Aunt Mina sighed. "And I think now we've seen some of those feelings escape."

"Something like this would upset anybody," said James softly. "Whatever age they might be."

"It might not be VHD," Mandy said hopefully. "All Mom said for certain was that we should get Pixie checked right away."

"I just had a horrible thought," said James. "If it *is* Alf spreading the disease, what if she infected other rabbits at the show?"

"We can't think like that," Mandy told him. "We'll take Pixie to the vet and tell them everything we know, and let the vet worry about what to do next."

"All right," said Aunt Mina. She glanced worriedly up the stairs. "I have to talk with Nadia and show her that this is the right thing to do. Mandy, could you put Pixie in his carrying case?"

Mandy nodded.

"Wait a minute!" said James. "Barry gave you Rachel's phone number, remember? Aunt Mina, can I call her and see if Alf's all right?"

"Of course," said Aunt Mina as she went upstairs.

"Good thinking," said Mandy. She thrust a hand into her jeans pocket and pulled out the scrap of paper. "Here it is. Call her, James, while I get Pixie." With Nadia out of the way, she could look at the little rabbit properly.

She knelt on the patio and rested Pixie on her lap. But when she tried to stroke his head, the rabbit twisted around as if he were trying to bite her.

Mandy flinched. She turned Pixie around and tried petting his back. He made no response.

"Mandy," James said breathlessly, running out onto the patio. "Alf has had the VHD vaccination! She couldn't have passed it on to Pixie or anyone!"

"That's fantastic news!" cried Mandy. Then she felt her heart sink. "But Pixie could still have caught it from one of the other rabbits."

"I suppose so," James agreed, his face falling. "I wonder how many of them have had the vaccination?"

"They were all so lovely," Mandy sighed, stroking Pixie. "Roly and Poly and Princess Powderpuff . . ."

"She's not just a rabbit, she's a *lagomorph*, remember?" said James sarcastically. "She's probably too fancy to get ill."

Suddenly, Pixie yanked his head away from Mandy's touch. "You wake up a bit when I do that, don't you?" she mused, studying him.

"'*Lagomorphs* have different teeth and everything,'" James continued, as if he was trying to cheer up Mandy with his impersonation of Angelica's snooty voice, "'and I should know because I'm *so* smart.'"

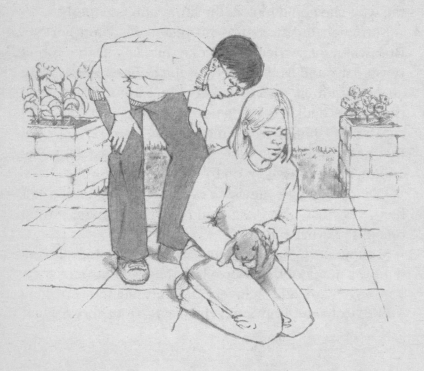

Mandy froze. "What did you say?"

"I'm so smart?"

"Before that," Mandy said urgently.

"About lagomorphs and their different teeth?" James shrugged. "It's just what Angelica said."

"But that could be it!" Mandy brushed her fingers against the top of Pixie's small furry head where his ears began, and Pixie didn't move. But when her fingertips strayed close to the side of his sweet little face, he squeaked and pulled away. He'd done that yesterday, too. Mandy remembered the way Pixie had sniffed the dandelion leaves before giving up on them — like something was stopping him.

Hardly daring to believe what she was seeing, she turned to ask James for his opinion. But just then, Aunt Mina appeared at the patio doors with Nadia. The girl looked pale and drawn, with red puffy eyes.

"I have the car keys," said Aunt Mina. "What's going on here?"

"Teeth!" Mandy cried excitedly. "Maybe it's not as bad as we thought. Maybe there's just something wrong with Pixie's teeth!"

Nadia stared at her in amazement. "His *teeth*?" She ran over and knelt beside Mandy. "You mean he's got a toothache?"

"Maybe. That could explain why he's been avoiding

food, couldn't it?" Mandy tried to raise Pixie's top lip to look at his mouth, but the little rabbit wriggled fretfully and twisted his head away. "Or maybe his teeth have just grown too long. Has he ever had a piece of wood in his cage to gnaw on, to keep them trimmed?"

"No," Nadia admitted. "I didn't know he needed one."

"Well, his front teeth don't look too bad," Mandy said. "But I can't see his cheek teeth at all." She turned to Nadia. "Do you think there is some inflammation there, around his face?"

Nadia peered closely, then nodded.

"I think we should go to the vet's right now," Aunt Mina said quickly, "and find out for sure what's going on."

The clinic was only a couple of miles away, but to Mandy, the tense, silent journey seemed ten times longer.

Luckily, the clinic wasn't busy. Besides a collie with a bandaged leg and a gray parrot in a cage that was almost as large as his elderly owners, they were the only ones in the waiting room.

"You two must think I'm a terrible pet owner," said Nadia, turning to look at Mandy and James.

"Don't be silly," Mandy said. "Anyone can see how much you love Pixie."

Nadia sighed. "I use flea spray in his cage to protect him from myxomatosis. I groom him and bathe him to keep him looking nice. But I didn't know about his teeth or this VHD thing. Maybe if I did, we wouldn't be here now."

"You can't learn everything about animals from books," James told her.

"I guess not. I'm — " Nadia paused. "I'm sorry I was such a pain, Mandy. If I'd let you take a good look at Pixie sooner, you might have seen this coming." She sniffed. "It's just that I don't like to feel there are things I can't deal with by myself."

Mandy put her hand on Nadia's arm. "That's what friends are for," she said. "Sharing problems and dealing with them together."

Nadia gave Mandy a teary smile. "Thanks."

"Mrs. Hunter?" said the receptionist, a large, red-faced woman. "Dr. Rogers will see you now."

"Here we go," Nadia said bravely.

"Together," James reminded her.

Dr. Rogers was a lanky gray-haired man with eyes as bright as his cheerful outlook. Once the introductions were out of the way, he took the case from Nadia and opened it.

"Who's this little fellow?" asked Dr. Rogers, peering inside.

"He's my pet," said Nadia quickly. "His name's Pixie, and he might have VHD."

"Well, I certainly hope he doesn't," said Dr. Rogers. "Let's have a look at him."

As he began to examine Pixie, Nadia described the rabbit's symptoms. Mandy couldn't help chipping in.

"Mom did say VHD was only a possibility," she pointed out. "She'd just dealt with a bad case where twenty-four rabbits had to be put down."

Dr. Rogers raised his bushy eyebrows. "Is your mother a vet?"

"And my dad," Mandy told him. "They run a practice in Welford."

"Animal Ark!" The vet beamed. "So you're Emily and Adam Hope's daughter, are you?"

She smiled. "That's right. I'm Mandy."

"I sat at their table at a veterinary dinner a few years back," he said. "Fine people — and a fine practice, too, I've heard."

"Mandy thought there might be something wrong with Pixie's teeth," said Nadia.

"There might very well be," said Dr. Rogers. "There's some facial swelling, and if he's been exhibiting signs of dysphagia . . ."

"What's that?" asked James.

"It means he wants to eat but can't." He lifted Pixie up. "Hmm, yes — bad breath. That's another sign."

"Can't you just look at his teeth?" asked Aunt Mina.

Dr. Rogers shook his head. "Unfortunately, the buccal folds — the baggy places around his cheeks — make it almost impossible to see his cheek teeth without sedating him." He carefully placed Pixie back on the examination table. "But I think it's important we have a good look."

"You won't put him to sleep, will you?" Nadia asked fearfully.

"Only a short snooze," said Dr. Rogers. "He'll be fine as long as we can check out those teeth and do something about them if necessary."

"Have I been feeding him wrong?" said Nadia, looking utterly dejected.

"No, not at all. Lop-eared breeds tend to suffer most from tooth trouble, I'm afraid," the vet explained.

"It all seemed to happen so quickly," said Aunt Mina. "One moment he was fine, the next . . ."

Dr. Rogers nodded sympathetically. "Well, rabbit teeth do grow at an amazing rate, as much as two or three millimeters every week."

Nadia looked stunned, and James's eyebrows shot up.

"So it's not VHD?" Nadia checked.

"I'm almost certain it's not," said Dr. Rogers.

The room erupted into cheers, and Mandy and Nadia hugged each other.

"What a relief," cried Mandy. "I'm sorry for scaring everyone by mentioning VHD at all."

"Don't be sorry," said Dr. Rogers. "VHD is something that rabbit owners need to be aware of. I recommend that Pixie get his inoculation as soon as I've filed his teeth."

"Definitely," agreed Aunt Mina. "When will you be able to treat him?"

"This afternoon." Dr. Rogers smiled at them all. "If you'd like to leave him here with me, I'll call you and let you know when he's ready to go home. I'll probably keep him overnight, if that's OK."

"Of course," said Aunt Mina.

"Thank you for looking after him," said Nadia, her eyes shining. She blew a kiss at Pixie, all small and snuggled in the vet's hands. Then, after a long, lingering look, she took her mom's hand and left the room.

"Give my regards to your parents, Mandy," said Dr. Rogers.

"I will," said Mandy. "And give Pixie a hug from me when he wakes up."

"We'll be keeping our fingers crossed that everything goes well," James added.

"Don't worry," said Dr. Rogers with a broad smile. "I'm sure it will. You did the right thing in bringing him to see me."

Nine

The next morning, Mandy, James, and Nadia decided to see if Herring needed another walk. They all wanted a distraction — Pixie was due to be picked up at twelve o'clock, and the waiting was unbearable.

"If anyone can take our minds off Pixie, it's Herring," said James.

"Oh, I can't wait to have my bunny back safe and sound again," said Nadia. "He *will* be all right, won't he, Mandy?"

"When we called the clinic last night, Dr. Rogers said the tooth filing was a success," Mandy reminded her.

"He only kept Pixie there to make sure he was able to eat properly again."

"And now it sounds like he's eating them out of house and home!" James smiled.

"Mom says she's going to buy some special scales," said Nadia as they reached the Maynards' front drive. "Then we can weigh Pixie each week. If he starts losing weight again, we'll realize in time and take him back to the vet's."

"That's a great idea," said Mandy. "And if you leave the inside of a toilet paper roll and some wood in his hutch, he can chew on them whenever he wants. That should help keep those runaway rabbit teeth under control!"

"What sort of wood should I use?" Nadia looked worried. "I don't want to give him something poisonous."

Mandy smiled sympathetically at Nadia. Clearly, her confidence in rabbit owning had been badly shaken. "Anything deciduous should be fine," she said. "From the older part of the tree, not fresh growth."

Nadia noticed a small stick lying by the side of the driveway, underneath a sycamore tree. "Like this one?"

"Oh, yes," said James. "Blackie loves chewing sycamore sticks. They last him a long time."

"You can't blame yourself for what happened to Pixie," Mandy told Nadia. "You love him and take great care of him. He couldn't have a kinder owner. Now that you know about his teeth, you won't let it happen again."

"For sure," Nadia vowed.

As they approached the Maynards' house, they almost bumped into Mrs. Maynard walking the other way with Herring.

"We were just coming to take him for a walk," James told her.

"Great minds think alike," she said, and laughed.

Herring strained against his leash, his shaggy tail wagging furiously, trying to say hello to them. But Mrs. Maynard produced the treat box from her pocket and shook it.

"Heel, Herring!" she ordered.

At once, Herring stopped tugging on the leash and sat down obediently.

"Good dog," said Mrs. Maynard. She opened the container and fed him a piece of jerky, which he gulped down.

"Well, treat-box training seems to be working well," said Mandy.

"He's getting the hang of it," Mrs. Maynard agreed happily. "Would you three like to take over? There are a hundred and one things I need to do today before the great Easter bunny judging this evening."

"Oh, no! I completely forgot about the contest!"

gasped Nadia. "Mandy, do you think Pixie will be all right to enter?"

"We'll have to wait and see," said Mandy. "He might not be feeling up to being on display."

Mrs. Maynard's face creased with concern. "What happened?"

Nadia told her the story, and Mrs. Maynard nodded sympathetically. "Well, I'll understand if you can't come this evening, and I hope Pixie gets well soon." She handed Herring's leash to James, gave Mandy the treat box and waved them off. "Good luck with the red flash there! See you later!"

"Let's go to the park again," James suggested.

"Good idea," said Mandy. "We can walk along the city wall like last time." She looked down at Herring, walking obediently beside her. "You'll like that, won't you, boy?"

James grimaced. "I just hope Angelica Angell's not in her yard this time, still going on about her perfect lagomorph."

"So *that's* where you learned the word," said Nadia. "How typical of Angelica to know something like that."

"It was James mentioning the word on the patio that made me think about Pixie's teeth," said Mandy. "Maybe if we see Angelica, we should thank her."

"Like her head needs to get any bigger," grumbled James.

As it turned out, Angelica was in her yard just like before, and certainly, her conversation was very similar.

"I can't wait for Princess Powderpuff to win the contest tonight," she was saying. "The moment the judges see her, she'll put all those ordinary nonpedigree rabbits in their place — *last* place!"

One of her friends snorted with laughter. "Good one, Angelica."

"Powderpuff's the best-bred rabbit for miles," said another.

Nadia frowned and broke away from Mandy, James, and Herring. They quickly set off after her.

"Are you all right?" Mandy asked.

"Angelica drives me crazy," Nadia replied glumly. "She's like that at school, too. All she cares about is showing off. Like winning is all that matters."

"I used to think you were a bit like that," James admitted. "But now I know I was wrong."

Nadia gave him a half smile. "Sure, I like being first in things, who wouldn't? But the best prize I could have is Pixie feeling better again."

Herring barked, making them all jump.

"Herring agrees!" Mandy joked. "Come on. Let's walk him once around the park. By the time we get back it'll be time to pick up Pixie."

* * *

They came back from the park with leaves and weeds poking out from every pocket. James had had the idea for a welcome-home feast in Pixie's honor, and on their trip around the park they had gathered up as many different tasty plants as they could find.

Aunt Mina poured them all some lemonade when they came through the door. "Did you have fun?" she asked.

"We did," said Nadia, pulling greenery from her pockets and placing it on the drain board. "And so did Herring."

Mandy nodded. "Whenever he tried to run off, we just shook the treat box and he came trotting right back."

Aunt Mina smiled and passed around the drinks. "Almost time to get Pixie," she said as she checked her watch. "Who wants to come?"

"Me!" Nadia said immediately.

"We'll stay here and get Pixie's feast ready," Mandy offered. "We need to wash all those leaves we just picked." She nudged James. "Don't we, James?"

"Er — yes!" He looked a little surprised. "Absolutely!"

"Are you sure?" Nadia asked. "Maybe you guys should come, too."

Mandy shook her head. "You're his owner, Nadia. Now go on! You can't keep Pixie waiting."

Nadia smiled uncertainly. "OK, see you soon."

As Nadia and her mom called their good-byes, James

frowned at Mandy. "What's the matter? Don't you want to see Pixie right away?"

"Of course I do," Mandy said. "But I think it's important for Nadia to get back her confidence in handling Pixie by herself."

James nodded. "Good thinking," he said. "Well, we'd better get on with the leaves. You wash, I'll dry."

"Fine," said Mandy. "Wait — the leaves don't *need* drying!"

"Really?" James asked innocently. But he couldn't keep a smile from spreading over his face.

Together, they carefully washed their rabbit party food and left it to drain.

"Why don't we clean out Pixie's hutch, too?" Mandy suggested. "So it's nice and clean when he comes back."

"A fresh start," James agreed.

They used a trowel to scrape out the old bedding and replaced it with fresh sawdust. While Mandy scrubbed out the inside of the water bottle with a wire brush, James took a bundle of hay and carefully shook the seeds from it, to keep them from getting into Pixie's eyes.

As Mandy was dropping the soiled litter into a garbage can, she heard a car pull up outside. "James," she called. "I think they're back!"

She and James rushed inside just as the front door opened.

"Welcome home!" they chorused.

"He looks so much better," Nadia declared, gently setting down Pixie's carrying case. "It's unbelievable. You'd hardly know he'd been sick!"

"That Dr. Rogers is a miracle worker," agreed her mom.

"Thanks for doing the leaves," said Nadia. "Let's take them outside and celebrate Pixie's return."

Mandy was thrilled to see that Nadia hadn't been exaggerating Pixie's recovery. He looked less scrawny already. His caramel-and-chocolate-flecked fur was more lustrous, and his black eyes were bright and clear again. If you looked closely there was still a slight swelling on the side of his face, but it wasn't enough to stop him from tearing into the pile of chickweed James had put down for him.

"And I've decided," said Nadia. "I want to take him to the Easter bunny judging tonight."

"Are you sure?" said Mandy.

Nadia nodded. "Dr. Rogers said it would be OK." She paused, and once Pixie had finished chewing a spindly strand of weed she picked him up. "I think I've been a bit overprotective of Pixie in the past. Judging by the way he's bounced back from this, I think he's tougher than I realized." Carefully, she passed him over to Mandy. "And life is for living, even when you're a rabbit. Right?"

Mandy placed Pixie in the crook of her arm and stroked his back. He looked up at her, his little nose twitching curiously. "Right," she said, and grinned.

"Would you help me get him ready?" asked Nadia. "We could bathe him together and then groom him."

"We've cleaned out his hutch, too," said James. "So he won't get dirty while he's waiting for the big event to start."

"Thank you," said Nadia. "Come on, guys, let's make this competition a real team effort!"

They spent the rest of the afternoon pampering the lop-eared bunny. With a bowl of warm water and some cotton pads, they gently bathed Pixie all over while he sat quietly munching a leaf. Then they took him inside to the living room. James held a small hair dryer at a safe distance, and while it blew warm air on a low setting, Mandy and Nadia brushed and stroked Pixie's fur, paying particular attention to his gorgeous long ears.

James switched off the hair dryer with a flourish. "He looks fantastic," he declared. "Almost as fluffy as Princess Powderpuff!"

"I don't care if he wins or loses," said Nadia. "I just

want to take part." She turned to James. "And I have another reason for wanting to go. Will you put Pixie back in his hutch for me? I need Mandy to help me with something."

"Sure," said James, picking up Pixie.

"What's up?" asked Mandy, following Nadia to her bedroom on the second floor.

Nadia switched on her computer. "I want to make some posters warning people about VHD," she explained. "Then we can take them to the contest and see if Mrs. Maynard will let us put them up around the hall, so all the rabbit owners can see."

"That's a great idea," said Mandy. "We can put the address of Dr. Rogers's clinic on it. Then anyone who hasn't had their rabbit vaccinated can go right there."

"Will you help me with the wording?" Nadia asked.

Mandy smiled. "I'd love to. Thanks for asking me."

By the time they'd finished designing and printing out the posters, it was nearly six o'clock. Mandy, James, and Nadia bundled into Aunt Mina's car, with Pixie snug and secure in his carrying case.

"I wonder if Alf will be there," said James.

"I hope so," Mandy said. "It would be nice to see her again."

"But not Herring," said Nadia. "He's great in a park, but not in a room full of rabbits."

Soon the air was filling with the scent of chocolate. A few minutes later, the factory came into sight. A sign had been put up next to the entrance: EASTER BUNNY CONTEST FINALS. Mandy felt a flutter of nerves in her tummy.

Sam and Jenny Maynard greeted them at the door to the hall. "Hello," said Mrs. Maynard. "So Pixie made it after all! I'm so happy for you."

"He's much better," Nadia agreed, producing the posters from her bag. "Do you think we could put some of these up around the hall?"

Mrs. Maynard scanned the pieces of paper and nodded approvingly. "An excellent idea," she said. "I'll tell you what. Why don't we give these to our judges to hand to each rabbit owner in person? Just to make sure the message gets across."

"That would be wonderful!" said Mandy.

"No problem," she said. "Ah, here's Suzie. She'll take you to your show table."

The show assistant approached them, all smiles. "Would you like to come this way? There's a name tag for you to fill in, like before."

They followed her through the hall. The show tables were laid out in four rows of five; not everyone had arrived yet, so several were unoccupied. Mandy noticed that the tables had been covered in green baize, and commented to Suzie.

"We had that done so that the rabbits would have something warm to sit on," she explained. "Better than the sawdust we used last time, and if they get skittish they won't slip around so much."

"Well, your contestants seem to appreciate it!" said Mandy. She could see all sorts of rabbits sitting calmly on their tables, their owners' hands cupped protectively around them or feeding them sprigs of greenery.

Suzie steered them to an empty table at the end of the second row, and James groaned when he spotted their neighbor. "Oh, no! What luck to be put next to Angelica Awful!"

Angelica Angell glanced scornfully at them as they approached. She was wearing an immaculate white suit with two matching white barrettes in her hair.

"Er, nice outfit, Angelica," said Nadia.

Angelica arched an eyebrow. "It's a perfect match for my perfect puff ball," she explained. "When the press takes our pictures with the winner's trophy, we'll look fabulous!"

"I can't believe she's accessorizing with her rabbit," Mandy whispered.

Nadia stifled a giggle. "I'm surprised she hasn't sewn a fluffy tail on the back of her pants!"

The two girls took Pixie from his case and prepared him for the judging. Mandy stroked him gently. With his

fluffy, newly washed fur helping to hide some of the weight he had lost, Pixie looked better than she had ever seen him.

"Hey, look!" said James, pointing to a table across the hall. "There's Rachel. She's got Alf with her."

"You two go and say hello," Nadia told them. "I'll give Pixie a pep talk."

"I think he'd prefer some groundsel," teased Aunt Mina.

"Hi, Rachel!" said Mandy, leading James over to Alf's table. "Hello, Alf!"

The dwarf rabbit's velvety ears were standing up straighter than ever. Her eyes were like big black buttons, and her pink nose twitched adorably.

"We really hoped you would come," said James.

"Barry talked me into it," Rachel admitted. "Told me there was nothing to worry about. 'Lightning doesn't strike in the same place twice,' he said." She smiled and ran a hand through her frizzy red curls. "But do *Herrings* strike twice, that's what I'd like to know!"

"Sorry I'm late," said a voice behind them. It was Barry, who produced a small striped box. "I've been busy working on the batch of these."

He opened the lid to reveal a cluster of creamy brown chocolates, decorated with delicate white stripes.

James's eyes widened, and his glasses slipped down his nose. "Are those the chocolates I invented?"

"You bet," grinned Barry. "The boss thinks they're delicious. He wants us to test them out tonight by handing one out to each owner and asking their opinion."

James took one of the offered chocolates. "I'll give you mine now," he said, popping the truffle in his mouth. "Mmmm, delicious!" he sighed. "Eleven out of ten!"

"What are you going to call them?" asked Mandy, taking one herself.

"Well, Sam's been calling them Jolly Jims," said Barry, winking at James. "And I think the name might stick."

James looked like all his Christmases had come at once. "That's amazing!" he cried. Then his face fell. "But what if no one else likes them? These could be the only Jolly Jims ever made."

"I'd better pass them around," said Barry. "And put you out of your misery! Here, take some yourself. You can help hand them out if you like."

James eagerly grabbed a few chocolates. Then he and Mandy said good-bye to Alf and Rachel and crossed back over to Pixie's table.

"I wasn't expecting to find my taste in chocolates to be judged tonight alongside all these rabbits," James said worriedly.

Mandy took a bite of her Jolly Jim. "You have nothing to worry about," she told him. "These taste incredible!"

James offered a chocolate to Nadia and Aunt Mina, who both accepted.

"Unusual flavor," noted Aunt Mina.

"And very tasty!" Nadia added.

James noticed Angelica watching him, and shyly offered her one of the truffles.

"What are these?" she said, taking one. After taking a tiny mouthful she grimaced. "Oh, no, I can't eat that. Strawberry, fudge, and white chocolate together? No one's going to like that!" She carelessly tossed the chocolate over her shoulder.

James looked crestfallen. "Ignore her," Mandy mouthed to him.

Suddenly, Nadia stiffened. "Look! The judges are here!" She gestured toward the door where two men and two women, all sporting blue ribbons on their lapels, were talking to the Maynards.

Mandy leaned toward the little lop-eared rabbit. "This is it, Pixie. This is your big moment." She ran the tip of her finger along one soft, floppy ear. "Good luck!"

Ten

The judges split into two groups to look at the rabbits. It didn't seem to take them very long to work their way through the contestants this time. Mandy guessed that they still had their notes from Saturday's show to help them.

She watched two of the judges inspecting Alf in the front row of tables. The tiny blue-black dwarf was sitting proudly next to a sprig of groundsel. One of the judges handed over a piece of paper — Nadia's VHD poster, Mandy realized with a thrill — and Rachel politely accepted it, even though Alf had already been vaccinated.

On the next table, Princess Powderpuff was under scrutiny by the other judges. Mandy didn't recognize the woman, but the man was Mr. Northington, Barry's supervisor.

"We're next!" hissed Nadia. "Oh, no! Help!"

"Well, as you can see," Angelica was explaining loudly to the judges, "my Princess is just as fabulous now as she was on Saturday. I'm sure you'll reach the right decision."

"Yes, I'm sure we shall," replied Mr. Northington.

The other judge, a slim blond woman with red glasses, produced one of Nadia's posters. "May I give you this? It's warning about VHD. Has your rabbit been inoculated?"

"I think Mommy took care of that," Angelica said airily. "But it doesn't matter if she didn't. Princess Powderpuff doesn't mix with common rabbits, so she won't catch anything."

"That's not a very good attitude to take toward your pet's welfare," said the woman as she inspected Princess Powderpuff. "I suggest you talk to your parents about getting this lovely animal protected as soon as —" She broke off with a cry and snatched her hand away. "Ouch!"

"What did you do to Princess Powderpuff?" Angelica demanded.

"What did *she* do to *me*, you mean," retorted the woman. "She bit my finger!"

Mandy, Nadia, and James all swapped incredulous looks. "That won't get her extra points," Nadia whispered.

"You upset Princess Powderpuff!" said Angelica. "Scaring her with talk of nasty common rabbit diseases!"

The judge examined her finger and then made an ominously long note on her clipboard. "Good-bye," she told Angelica frostily. Then she and Mr. Northington moved away.

"No! Come back and look at her again!" Angelica called after them. "Look, if it makes you feel better, I *know* that Mommy made the vet give Princess Powderpuff that injection." But when she saw that the judges were ignoring her, she sat down angrily on the chair behind her table.

"So, this is Pixie, is it?" Mr. Northington smiled as he approached Nadia's table.

"That's right," said Nadia. "He hasn't been very well, I'm afraid."

"I'm sorry to hear that," said the female judge, producing one of the posters. "On that worrying subject, may I give you one of these?"

"Actually, we wrote it," Nadia told her shyly. "We had

quite a scare, even though Pixie didn't have VHD after all, and we wanted to save other people from going through the same thing."

"What a good idea," said the judge. "Many of the owners here didn't even know about VHD until they read this." She lowered her voice. "And I must confess that neither did I! I'm having my little Barnaby inoculated as soon as possible!"

Mandy and Nadia smiled at each other.

"Now then, Pixie, let's have a look at you," said Mr. Northington. Pixie sniffed the air and took a few cautious steps toward him across the green felt table covering. "He's a curious little fellow, isn't he?"

"Yes, he is," said Nadia.

Suddenly, Pixie hopped closer and put both his front paws on Mr. Northington's arm. He propped himself up and looked at the judge, his little nose twitching adorably.

"Well, he's a very handsome rabbit," said the female judge, making some brief notes on her checklist. Suddenly, Pixie squeaked and hopped down from Mr. Northington's arm. As he did so, he dropped his head sideways so that one of his lop ears brushed against the table top, spreading out like a paddle of caramel-colored velvet.

"He's not just handsome — he's quite the performer!" said Mr. Northington, laughing.

A few moments later, the judges moved on to the next table. Nadia looked anxious. "I hope they liked him!"

"Pixie showed himself off very well," Mandy assured her. "That thing he did with his ear was so cute!"

"He hasn't done that since he was a baby," Nadia said fondly. "Oh, it's so good to see him well again!"

"I wonder how my Jolly Jims are doing," said James. He was watching Barry hand out the trial chocolates.

"Are you nervous?" asked Mandy sympathetically.

"Yes. I want to prove Angelica wrong — about my chocolates, as well as rabbits like Pixie!"

Nadia smiled. "Don't worry. I think we'll be fine after her little puff ball's behavior just now."

"Look," said Mandy, clutching Nadia's arm. "They're bringing out the Easter basket!" The wicker basket looked even more magnificent than she remembered.

"The judges are discussing, too," observed Aunt Mina. "It won't be long now before the winner is chosen."

"I hope not," said Nadia. "I can't stand the suspense!"

A few minutes later, the hall fell silent as Mrs. Maynard stepped onto the stage and tapped the microphone. A shrill whistle echoed over the loudspeakers, then her voice crackled out.

"Thank you all so much for coming back," she began. "Even though my dog is not around to provide some extra drama" — she paused for a low murmur of laughter — "it's been a very exciting evening."

People clapped and cheered.

"I'm sure you'll agree that every rabbit in this room is a winner," Jenny Maynard went on. "But there can only be one Merry's Easter Bunny this year." She gestured to the Easter basket beside her. "Only one rabbit will get to sit here, ready to be immortalized in chocolate!"

She pulled out a golden envelope, and a hush settled over the hall.

"But before I reveal the winner," she smiled, "there's something I need to ask. What did you all think of the chocolates that our Mr. Greenhalgh passed around?"

Immediately, a loud round of applause rang out.

"They're delicious!" called out a man from the back of the hall.

"Are they available yet?" asked a woman near the door.

James stared around, red faced but with a huge grin.

"I'm pleased to hear you like them," said Mrs. Maynard. "They're a new line, so watch for them in the shops soon."

"Well done, Jolly James!" cheered Nadia, and Mandy squeezed James's shoulder.

"And now, without further ado," Jenny Maynard announced, "here is our winner." She opened the envelope. "The Merry's Easter Bunny will be . . ."

Mandy closed her eyes and crossed her fingers.

". . . Pixie the Holland Lop!"

Nadia whooped with delight as everyone burst out clapping. Mandy and James grinned at each other, and Aunt Mina did her best to gather them all together for a giant hug. Mandy saw Rachel and Barry waving and giving them a big thumbs-up, while Angelica fixed Nadia with a furious stare. But Pixie himself sat unfazed on his green table, far more interested in chewing the last piece of groundsel than in the fuss being made about him.

"The judges wanted a rabbit who was curious, friendly, and happy." Jenny Maynard grinned. "And to the best of our knowledge, we've never made a lop-eared chocolate bunny, so Merry's will be giving this seasonal favorite a makeover!"

As a fresh wave of laughter and applause started up, Nadia put her hands to her face. "I can't believe it," she murmured. "I can't believe Pixie managed to win after all he's been through."

"Well, I think it's been fixed," Angelica said loudly. "Anyone can see that Princess Powderpuff is the best-bred rabbit here!" She turned around in a flounce to pick up her beloved rabbit, and Mandy, Nadia, and James burst out laughing.

Angelica turned around and narrowed her eyes at Nadia. "What's so funny?" she demanded.

"Have you seen the back of your pants?" spluttered Nadia.

Angelica looked down and gasped with horror. There was a sticky brown smear all over the seat of her dazzling white slacks. "My outfit!" she wailed. "It's ruined!"

"It's that Jolly Jim she threw away," James realized. "She must have sat on it!"

Sputtering with fury, her cheeks burning crimson, Angelica scooped up Princess Powderpuff and stomped out of the hall.

"Well, *that* little outburst is out of the way," Mrs. Maynard went on. "May I please welcome the winners onstage so that the first photographs of our new Easter bunny can be taken? Ladies and gentlemen, may I present Pixie — escorted by her owner, Nadia Hunter!"

There were more cheers, and the loudest applause yet, as Nadia proudly carried Pixie up to the stage. And as she placed him carefully in the basket, no one was cheering and whistling louder than Mandy and James.

That night, Aunt Mina prepared a celebratory Romanian feast. There were plenty of cheeses and soups — *ciorba taraneasca*, a vegetable soup, was Mandy's favorite — and a fantastic quichelike dish, cut in squares and served in cabbage leaves. Mandy and James both agreed they'd never seen so much food in their lives, and when the feast was over they crawled to bed full and content.

The rest of the vacation passed quickly: walking Herring, whose attention problem seemed to have been solved completely thanks to James's treat box invention, playing with prizewinning Pixie, and getting excited about the big presentation on Saturday afternoon.

"Mr. Maynard must be pushing his workers very hard to have the Pixie-shaped mold made in time," Mandy reflected, running a brush over Pixie's agouti fur.

"I hope the finished bunnies look just like him," said Nadia.

"They took photos of him from every possible angle," James reminded her. "So they have plenty of reference material."

Nadia turned to Mandy. "I'm really glad your dad agreed to wait until the presentation was over before taking you both home," she said.

"He *had* to agree." Mandy grinned. "We wouldn't miss Pixie's big moment for anything!"

The little rabbit kept eating and eating like he was making up for lost time, and by the time Saturday came around, he was almost back to health. As Aunt Mina took them to the factory for the presentation, Mandy felt a twinge of sadness that she and James would soon be going home.

"This has been a wonderful vacation," she declared. "Thanks for everything, Mrs. Hunter."

"I'm glad you've enjoyed yourselves," said Aunt Mina as she parked the car. "It's been quite a week, with one thing or another!"

"You can say that again!" replied James from the front seat.

Mandy turned to Nadia, who was holding Pixie's case on her lap. "I'm going to miss you," she said. "And Pixie, too."

"Perhaps we can come to see you during midterm break?" Nadia suggested hopefully.

"That would be great," said Mandy. "I'd love to show you Animal Ark."

Nadia grinned. "Thanks. And in the meantime, you'll be able to see Pixie anytime you like — on his Merry's chocolate wrapper!"

Mrs. Maynard was waiting to greet them. She had some paperwork for Aunt Mina to sign, allowing them to use Pixie's image on packaging and even on some specially made mugs. Then, Mandy, James, and Nadia were ushered around the back of the main factory building toward the hall.

"Where's Herring today?" asked James.

"Waiting with Suzie outside," said Mrs. Maynard. "See?"

Mandy smiled when she saw Herring sitting meekly beside Suzie just outside the door, as journalists and Merry's workers drifted in and out of the hall.

"Thanks to you, we've got him eating out of the palm of our hands," said Jenny Maynard happily. "Well, out of the treat box, anyway! Now, come and meet Pixie's chocolate double."

Mandy and James followed Nadia into the hall, and instantly a dozen flashbulbs popped in their faces as photographers scrambled to take pictures.

"Look!" cried Mandy, blinking away the bright lights in her eyes and pointing to the enormous basket of goodies. She felt a flash of sympathy for pop stars. "There it is!"

She and Nadia rushed forward to see. Sure enough, there was a life-size chocolate Pixie wrapped in shiny gold foil. Nadia set down the carrying case and lifted Pixie out.

"That's amazing!" said James, peering at the chocolate rabbit, then glancing at Pixie to compare it with the real thing. The detail was incredible — it looked more like a sculpture in stone than a hollow chocolate model. Every feature, from his gorgeous long ears, to his small fluffy tail, had been lovingly captured.

"I hope you're pleased," said Jenny Maynard. Mandy realized that she was as anxious about having their approval as Nadia had been during the judging.

"We're thrilled!" said Nadia. "Aren't we, Pixie?" She set Pixie down opposite his chocolate image. The little rabbit sniffed at his foil-wrapped neighbor, then gave a tiny bunny shrug as if he knew it wasn't real. Mandy and James stood to one side as the photographers crowded in for more pictures.

"There are miniature Pixies, too," Mrs. Maynard

explained, passing a small foil-wrapped chocolate bunny to them.

"It's exactly like Pixie!" said Mandy, looking at the wrapper. "He looks so sweet!"

"The charities can't wait to receive their special baskets," Jenny Maynard went on. "We're distributing them today. Lots of them are being raffled off at Easter parties this weekend." She took a small striped box from the big basket. "And there will be one of these in each of them!"

James read the label. "Jolly Jims!" he exclaimed.

"The first batch," she informed him. "We'll be selling them locally at first, and if they take off they'll go nationwide."

Mandy clapped her hands. "Next time you visit Nadia, maybe you'll invent a whole new chocolate bar, James!"

The photographers had retreated once they had their pictures, and Nadia was left staring proudly at the basket of Easter goodies. Pixie was perched on the straw next to his chocolate counterpart.

James's eyes gleamed. "Best of all, we get to take that giant chocolate bunny home," he said greedily.

"It's so much like the real Pixie I'm not sure I can eat it," admitted Nadia.

"Well, you can always have a Jolly Jim instead," said Mandy, offering her a chocolate.

Nadia grinned and showed the sweet to Pixie. "What do you think of this, boy?"

Pixie hopped across the straw, over the rim of the basket, and scampered over to the doorway of his carrying case. There he started gnawing hungrily on the piece of wood that Mandy had popped in with him. Obviously, he preferred that to the thought of a squishy white chocolate-fudge-strawberry fondant combination.

Mandy laughed. "Well, to each his own, Pixie," she said, stroking the world's first lop-eared Easter bunny. His fur was softer than ever, and his ears felt like velvet. "And it's great to see you'll be taking care of your own teeth from now on!"